# PROJECT AIDA

MICHAEL ABOLINS

EMLIN
PRESS

First Published in Great Britain 2025 by Emlin Press



ISBN (eBook) 978-1-914473-97-5

ISBN (Print) 978-1-914473-98-2

ISBN (Audiobook) 978-1-914473-99-9

A CIP catalogue record for this book is available from the British Library.

www.emlinpress.com

*For all those who push me to be better.*

# ONE

My name is Wilbur Brooke.

You can call me Mister Brooke. I acknowledge this interview is being recorded.

I'm fifty-six years old. Date of birth is twelfth of August, nineteen ninety-four.

I don't know what my National Insurance number is, not off the top of my head.

I live in apartment 336, St. James Hamlets, London Road.

If by "owner", you mean the person she provides care services for, yes.

I'm not her "owner". She's not an appliance.

She's an Ella.

An E-L-A. Ella.

Enhanced Living Assistant.

I am the legally registered keeper of Ella serial number… 83845-RJ. Funny what you remember.

Eight or nine months ago. I didn't buy her. I said "her", not "it," that's correct.

Leased, I suppose.

Yes, I picked her. It was like buying a car. Strange, really.

I'm uncomfortable talking about it with you, in particular.

It was an MVA voucher scheme. Ministry for Veteran's Affairs. I couldn't afford her otherwise.

I applied because of my mobility. This leg's artificial. This leg's wracked with arthritis. I think I'd fallen something like three or four times in the previous six months. I live on my own. I don't have any family. I needed someone to help out around the house. Someone who could call an ambulance, should the worst happen.

I don't require any specialised assistance right now, no.

Physio. Quality-of-life stuff, things like that. Round-the-clock care.

I was means-tested. A residential health assessment. Due to my living situation, some bureaucrat somewhere rubber-stamped it. I don't know. I was surprised to be approved, to be honest. You'd have to ask the MVA if you wanted to know more.

I served from twenty-nineteen to twenty-thirty-seven. Honourable discharge due to injury. Yes, the leg.

Hainan Island.

Have you served?

No, thought not.

TWO

It looks for all the world like an upmarket coffee bar. The lighting is bright. The décor bland yet inviting, a narrow mix of beige and light brown hues. It doesn't make Wilbur feel any more comfortable stepping through the sliding glass door. Nor does the wall of cool aircon he walks into.

He pauses, the door hissing closed behind him. He pushes his hand in and out of his pocket and forces a smile at the young man already approaching him, hand extended.

'Good afternoon, sir, welcome to Autonomi Industries. My name's Brett, how can I help you today?'

Wilbur cagily shakes Brett's hand, makes sure to squeeze firmly enough. He'd run through this conversation enough times in his head, yet he still stumbles over the first line. 'I'd, um, I'm here… I've got an MVA voucher.' Meek. Annoyed at himself already.

Brett takes it in his stride. 'Excellent, come, take a seat. We get gentlemen like you in here every now and again.' He shows Wilbur to a tan-coloured sofa, curving around a circular white coffee table with a potted plant in the centre of it.

Wilbur sits, shuffles along to avoid sitting at the very end.

'Can I get you something to drink? Maybe tea, coffee, or a glass of water?' Brett hovers, awaiting Wilbur's response.

'Coffee, please.' Then, pre-empting the next question, 'black'.

Brett nods, happy with purpose, and strides off.

Wilbur shifts on the sofa, tugs on his trouser legs, looks around. There are five other curved-sofa and circular coffee table assemblies in the bright, open space. Two are occupied with slightly uneasy couples talking to shiny young things. At a third, a handsome couple sit talking, clearly much more comfortable in each other's company and this space.

Brett returns, coffee in hand and tablet tucked under his arm. He hands the former to Wilbur, who grunts his thanks, then folds himself into the seat on Wilbur's left.

'Thanks for choosing Autonomi today, you won't regret it. As I said, I'm Brett, you are…'

'Wilbur. Wilbur Brooke.'

'I'm going to start, Wilbur, may I call you Wilbur?' Brett opens a page on his tablet, enters details. 'I'm going to ask a few basic questions, just so we can gauge your requirements.'

Brett asks questions, Wilbur answers questions, at times referring to the email on his smartphone before giving up and handing the device to Brett to crib from directly.

'Alright, Wilbur, your MVA voucher entitles you to our Silver package. It covers the entire monthly subscription, you've got nothing to worry about. We claim the costs directly from the MVA, you don't need to do a thing. Ok?' Wilbur nods, shouldn't be relieved but is. 'Ok. That includes the Ella unit itself, twenty-four-seven customer care for the first six weeks of the contract while you're settling in, and the standard warranty that lasts the length of the contract. It's pretty comprehensive, to be honest. The terms and conditions are here—' hands Wilbur the tablet, the screen a wall of dense text, '—and they only exclude what you'd expect. It doesn't cover violence perpetrated by yourself or, by your action, others against the Ella unit. It doesn't cover damage incurred as a result of deliberate misadventure or malice. Likewise, damage occurring as a result of negligence or misuse, as defined by the terms of the end-user license agreement, which you can read here—' Brett swipes on the tablet in Wilbur's hand, reveals another screen of small print '—isn't covered, either. In short, what that means is, if the unit is damaged under any of those circumstances, Autonomi Industries is entitled to pursue the associated costs from you directly, along with a penalty and possible repossession of the unit. I'm sure it won't come to that, Wilbur, but I always like to be transparent about these things. Make sure there's no grey areas, right?' Brett smiles, teeth white.

Wilbur nods, looks again at the tablet, the words not going in. Asks, 'Are they all called Ella?' Feels stupid when Brett laughs.

'No, no. That's just what we call them here. They're ee-el-ay's, ELAs, right? Enhanced Living Assistants. We call them Ellas for short.' Brett gets to his feet. 'Now, that's a lot to take in, Wilbur. What I'm going to do is leave you to read through it. I'll pop out back and go through our inventory, make sure everything's ready for you. I'll ask Alex and Jo to come over, they'll help you through all the tees and cees. It's important you understand them before you sign. It's not super-onerous or anything, we're not looking to catch you out, it's just to make sure everyone knows where they stand. Ok, I'll be back in ten minutes.'

Wilbur nods again, all he's done so far, then stares at the

screen. Looks up as the comfortable-looking couple approach from their sofa. They smile. Man and a woman, Wilbur can't tell who's Alex and who's Jo. Both dressed smart-casual, like catalogue models. Good-looking in a non-threatening way, like catalogue models.

'May we?' says the man, gesturing at the sofa.

Wilbur opens his mouth, then closes it, clears his throat. Tries again. 'Yes.' Worth the effort.

The man smiles kindly, waits for the woman to sit before he does. 'I'm Alex, this is Jo. We understand you're here under the MVA scheme?' Both of them staring intently at Wilbur as he replies.

'Yes, I got an email,' is all he can think to say, completely out of his depth.

Jo leans forward, a strand of her blonde hair falling from behind her ear. Places her hand on Wilbur's knee. 'First of all, let us thank you for your service. Everyone here at Autonomi is grateful.'

Wilbur instinctively leans away at her touch, not used to the contact. He's used to the sentiment, all right, but not the touch. The sentiment he hears all the time. Doesn't make it any more genuine. He gives the automatic 'Thank you,' and smile, like he appreciates they recognise what he gave up.

Another kind smile from Alex. 'We're here to help you through the sign-up process. Answer any questions you might have, either about the paperwork or about Ellas in general. I assume you're familiar with the basics?'

'Just about,' says Wilbur, anticipating what's coming next.

Jo's the one to ask. They leave it to the woman to ask the personal question. 'It's a live-in carer you need, is that right?' Her tone soft, caring. Maternal, almost.

'It is, yes. One leg prosthetic, the other rheumatoid arthritis,' says Wilbur, tapping his knees like he's checking she didn't do something to them. 'I don't get around as well as I used to.' Wilbur immediately gives them both credit for not making that twisted-mouth, tilted-head expression of pity. 'The doctor signed off on my grant application to the MVA a couple of weeks ago.'

Alex. 'It's great they didn't keep you waiting.'

'Tell me what I need to know,' says Wilbur, wanting an end to the small talk. 'Do they really expect me to read all this?' holding up the tablet to Alex.

'You can either read it, or we can talk you through the salient points. You need to sign at the bottom of the document regardless, and if you rely on us to talk you through it, I need you to give clear verbal acceptance that you're happy to rely on our spoken testimony.'

'Oh,' says Wilbur.

'It's quite all right,' says Alex. 'I know it seems intimidating, but it really isn't. Brett wasn't lying when he said no-one's trying to catch you out. Why don't you enjoy your coffee and let Jo and I take you through it?'

So that's what Wilbur does. Sips his coffee, stares into Alex's brown eyes, Jo's blue eyes, and listens. Tries to take in as much as he can. The coffee is surprisingly good. He asks them to repeat only a couple of points.

They get to the end. 'You sign here,' says Jo, leaning towards him and scrolling to the end of the first document on the tablet. Wilbur scribbles with his fingertip, then presses it to the fingerprint reader under the screen. 'And here.' Jo swipes, scrolls. Wilbur signs.

'And because you relied on Jo and I to talk you through the terms and conditions and the end-user license agreement on your behalf, can you please verbally confirm that you accept the aforementioned terms, conditions and agreement as described by Jo and I.'

'Yes, I do. I accept,' says Wilbur, feeling it's somehow inadequate. 'Is this being recorded? That you've read out those terms and I've said I accept them?' He looks up and sees the small security cameras positioned discretely in the corners of the showroom.

'Yes, both Jo and I have captured the moment.'

Wilbur is puzzled. Looks them over for a clip-on camera. Sees Jo's mouth open in an 'o' before she places her hand over it.

'Brett didn't tell you, did he?' says Jo.

Wilbur's mind catches up. 'You're…' Unsure what to call them.

'We're both Ellas,' says Jo. 'I'm sorry, usually Brett makes that clear. We weren't trying to mislead you, we genuinely thought you already knew.'

'That's ok, it's ok,' says Wilbur. 'I mean it, it's no problem.' He does mean it. 'I should have figured, really, shouldn't I? Is Brett…'

'He's human. It's company policy to always have at least one human member of staff on site. Right, do you have any questions about anything we've discussed so far?'

Wilbur says no. Mainly because his head is still spinning.

'When you're ready, tap the button on the screen and we'll set you up with your very own Ella.'

Wilbur returns his attention to the screen. A large button with text on it says *Welcome to your Autonomi Industries ELA*. Wilbur taps it, digital confetti flies on-screen. Two more buttons appear, one pale pink, says *Female*. One pale blue, says *Male*. Wilbur looks up, uncertain.

'You can choose your Ella from those in our inventory,

right here. Or, if we don't have the model you want today, we can ship it to your home address within five days.'

Wilbur, suddenly feeling awkward, lowers his eyes and stares at the screen.

It's like Jo can read him.

'It's fine to feel a little uneasy, Wilbur,' she says, using that maternal tone of voice again. 'Nearly all our male clients choose a female Ella. Most of our female clients do, too.'

'They do?' asks Wilbur.

'They do,' confirms Alex. The two Ellas share a look that says they don't suffer the same hang-ups. 'Both our male and female clients find the female Ella units to be more welcoming. Approximately 73% of the Ella units on a Silver subscription are female models. That's our male and female clients combined. There's a more even split at the Gold tier, male clients picking female Ella units, female clients picking male Ella units.'

Wilbur stares. Doesn't follow.

'Sexual recreation functionality is part of the Gold subscription tier,' says Jo, like she's describing a phone package.

Wilbur sits back, sorry he asked.

Jo smiles. 'We talk quite openly about our service levels. We might not advertise it, but it is part of Autonomi Industries' offering after all.' Most ordinary thing in the world.

'With the Silver, what would happen if...' Can't bring himself to finish the question he's ashamed to ask.

'The permissions that enable that functionality in Gold are locked down at Silver level. If you were to try, the Ella unit would prevent you. We are quite strong and each of us receives thorough self-defence training. Additionally, any attempt would be recorded, Autonomi would be notified, and the Ella unit would be retrieved, forcibly if necessary.'

'That was in the terms and conditions?'

'"The user is not permitted to perform any act or behaviour toward the Product not accommodated for at the user's current subscription level under punishment of fine, withdrawal of the Product at the Company's request, and criminal prosecution." We did cover that,' explains Jo. More patiently than she is entitled to be, thinks Wilbur.

Wilbur returns to the choice in front of him.

'Would you like us to leave you alone for a few minutes?' Jo again. The sensitive one.

Wilbur shakes his head, stabs at the *Female* button. The screen fades, two buttons replaced by eleven small portrait photos. A catalogue of catalogue models.

'These are all the models currently in our inventory here, today. You can deselect this box here,' Alex reaches over and taps the screen, 'to see the full range.'

Additional portraits fill the screen. A scroll bar on the side of the screen. Too much choice, too much pressure. Wilbur ticks the *Available today* box; the extra portraits disappear.

Alex and Jo sit back and share a look that, to Wilbur, appears to be pride. Like a proud married couple. He remembers how those looks felt.

Wilbur turns his attention to the screen, scans the faces staring back at him. White, Asian, Black, shades in-between. Blondes, brunettes. *Her*. Wilbur taps the portrait of the white female that catches his eye. Shoulder-length dark brown hair. The photo enlarges. She's of indeterminate age, somewhere between late-twenties and mid-thirties, if Wilbur had to guess. Details, measurements, specifications, options trickle down the screen. Looks… Perfect? Feels something twist in his gut.

'The physical specifications are set, you can't make any alterations to those. The personality traits and interests can be customised, though.' Alex speaks softly. Soothingly? Perceptive, Alex and Jo.

Wilbur can't meet their eyes right now. He scrolls, reads, finds it all too abstract. Like the video games he used to play as a youth. Stops at the first menu. *Choose five core personality traits.*

'These five are just a starting point. The Ella will grow and develop as it gets to know you better. As it adapts to how you would like it to interact with you. You can also simply ask it to dial up or down any aspect of its personality.'

'Do you mind if I ask you what personality tropes you two had selected?'

'Traits, not tropes.' Jo smiles. Somehow Wilbur doesn't feel patronised or admonished. 'Alex and I were initially configured to emphasise politeness, professionalism, confidence, helpfulness and friendliness. We've grown since, through additional training programs and our interactions with clients. It's our daily interactions with clients and other people that enables us to develop our uniqueness. Alex will encounter different experiences to me, for example. Those will shape his personality in ways that are individual to him.'

Wilbur reads through the list, little monochromatic lozenges containing words like *Creative, Driven, Insightful, Sympathetic*. Begins thinking. Selects *Confident*, thinks that someone in this situation will need to be. Selects *Friendly* on the basis he's sharing his home with them. Doesn't want to tiptoe around some cold fish.

'Isn't *Helpful* kind of the point?' Wilbur looks up at Alex and Jo.

'Think of it as how proactive you want them to be,' says

Alex. 'Your Ella's primary function is as a caregiver, tailored to your particular requirements. Being *Helpful* means they'll more actively look for other ways to offer assistance. Some people prefer to retain as much independence as they can.'

Makes sense. Selects *Trustworthy*, wonders again. 'That should be a given?'

'Of course.' Jo this time. 'All information collected by your Ella is encrypted and securely stored. Data that's shared with Autonomi Industries is likewise encrypted and any personal identifiers removed. *Trustworthy* in this instance refers to honesty and truthfulness, the extent to which you feel able to rely on your Ella with matters other than its primary function.'

Layers within layers, Wilbur thinks. Two more.

Selects *Empathic*, seems like a pretty fundamental characteristic you want in someone who's primary function is caregiver. One more. Scrolls back up and down the list.

'Does it need to be five?'

'No, but we recommend five as a good foundation. More than five, the traits can become too prescriptive, it doesn't leave enough room for individual development. You can leave it at four, but you might find that, occasionally, your Ella acts a bit like a blank slate if they don't have a full suite of personality traits to call upon in any given situation. It'll pass as they develop, but there would be a gap in their make-up to begin with.'

Wilbur low-level panics, selects *Adventurous* without being 100% sure why, sounds like it's good? Looks up at Alex and Jo. 'Interests?'

'Your interests shape you, don't you agree?' Asks Alex, leaning forward. 'Your hobbies, your pursuits, your passions help make you who you are. Not to mention, bring you joy, pleasure and satisfaction. Would you like to be able to share those interests with your Ella? Would you like your Ella to be interested in different subjects to you, maybe there's a pastime you've always wanted to master? A musical instrument you've always wanted to learn?'

'They're not as important as the personality traits, but we still recommend you select between three and five.' Jo chips in.

This is harder work than Wilbur was expecting. A greater responsibility than he had anticipated. Again, the lozenges. Plus, a text-entry box to add his own. Ok, he can do this. Selects *History*. *Health & fitness* can't hurt. *Mental health* doesn't sound like an interest as much as it does an occupation, selects it anyway. Taps *Music* and, at a loss, *Food*.

Jo and Alex smile as he completes his choices, prompt him to confirm them. He does. Jo leans forwards, hands clasped. 'This is it, Wilbur. Once you tap *Create Ella*, your choices will be sideloaded to the model you selected. Any last questions?'

Only how surreal this feels, thinks Wilbur. He remembers spending longer configuring a new car. 'No. No questions.'

He taps the button. The screen fills with the portrait of the Ella he chose, fades to black. Countdown timer starts, five minutes.

'That's it,' says Alex. 'Your choices will be sideloaded, integrated with the Ella's core system matrix, then tested. Then she'll be ready.'

'Do I need to go anywhere?' Wilbur is flustered by the seeming enormity of his choices.

'No, she'll—'

Brett re-appears, loud. 'Congratulations, Wilbur, I just saw your order come through on our system.' Slaps Wilbur on the back before sitting on the end of the sofa. 'I hope Alex and Jo are looking after you. Have they explained everything, answered all your questions?'

Wilbur suddenly feels protective of Alex and Jo, can't explain why. 'Yes, they were incredibly helpful.' Looks at them. 'Thank you, both.'

They, of course, smile bright smiles.

'I'm glad to hear it,' says Brett. 'We'll email you copies of all the documentation. You can also access it through the Autonomi Industries app on your phone, along with user guides, help and support, and a chat interface that you can use to communicate with your Ella if you or they are out of conversational range. And of course, you can always drop by and see us here. Isn't that right?' Brett looks at Alex and Jo. Prompting them like children, thinks Wilbur.

Alex and Jo simply keep smiling at Wilbur and nod their heads.

'There's a very active community on the Autonomi Industries subreddit and Discord server, too,' adds Brett. 'There are links in the app. But if I could give you one piece of advice, it would be to talk to your Ella. Ask questions, whatever's on your mind. There's no such thing as a stupid question and you'll find your Ella far less judgemental than most humans. Don't worry about feeling embarrassed or feeling awkward. Your Ella is here for you, remember. It's at your service. Ok?'

Wilbur, butterflies beginning to stir. 'Good advice, thank you.'

'It's my pleasure. While we wait, I just need to tell you a couple more things. Firstly, you'll receive an email this afternoon or this evening, asking how you found our service today. If you'd be so kind as to spend a few minutes completing the survey, it would go a long way to helping us understand what we're doing right and what we could be doing better. Secondly

—' ticking the points off on his fingers '—we'll also send you a special referral code. If you have any friends or family who are thinking about joining the Autonomi Industries family, give them the code. They can get their first three months free, and you'll get the cosmetics upgrade package free for your Ella for three months. The cosmetics package is just one of a range of monthly add-ons you can get to enhance your Ella. Again, you can find out more and add them to your subscription in the app. They renew monthly and you can cancel at any time.'

Something begins buzzing. Brett feels his pockets. 'That'll be me. Wilbur, will you please excuse me?' Doesn't wait for an answer. Doesn't ask Alex and Jo to excuse him. Gets up, presses the phone to his ear and departs, already talking to someone else.

'Is it usual to feel this nervous?' Needs to get it off his chest. Wipes his palms on his trouser legs.

'It's perfectly natural, Wilbur,' says Jo, kindness incarnate. 'Feels like a first date, right?'

'Yeah, it does. Been a long time,' says Wilbur, all anxious energy. Straightaway regrets agreeing with the comparison, wonders what that says about him. This isn't the Gold package, after all.

Alex. 'It's ok. You're inviting someone new into your life. I'd be concerned if you didn't feel nervous.'

Wilbur nods, twice, three times.

Alex looks over Wilbur's shoulder. 'Here she is.'

Wilbur practically leaps to his feet. Feels embarrassed, standing out like a sore thumb, not dressed catalogue nouveau like everyone else. His stomach somersaults. The woman whose portrait he pressed his finger to on the screen just minutes ago, walking towards the sofa. She smiles, they're all smiles here at Autonomi Industries, gives a little wave. Casual. Comfortable in her skin. Confident.

She reaches the coffee table. Alex and Jo slide along, a buffer between her and Wilbur. She sits, sweeping her long fawn skirt underneath her. Elegantly precise in her movements. Stretches out a hand to him. 'Wilbur, isn't it?' Like she doesn't already know all about him.

Wilbur takes her hand, tries to hide his trembling. Doesn't squeeze at all this time. 'Hi.' Feels like he needs to make a good first impression. 'How are you?' is all that comes to mind. Stupid.

'I'm well, thank you for asking,' she says.

'It's alright Wilbur, you can sit down.' Gentle Jo.

Wilbur flushes, sits, clears his throat.

Before he can compose the question, Jo speaks. 'You're probably wondering what happens now. Alex and I will leave you two alone so you can say your hellos. Once you're ready to leave, we'll have everything else you need waiting, and you can head home together.'

'Thank you, Jo,' she says. 'Thanks for looking after him for me, the both of you.' Did she really wink?

Wilbur, discombobulated, almost desperate, asks 'What's her, sorry—' Changes aim. 'I'm sorry, I don't know your name. There was no option.' Christ, Wilbur.

She's not fazed. 'It's fine Wilbur. Don't worry, you and I will discuss that shortly, along with a few other things.' She turns to Jo and Alex. 'Is there anything else I need to know right now?'

Alex shakes his head. 'You're up to speed. We'll leave you to it. Wilbur, remember: no pressure, no rush, you'll each learn about the other at your own pace.' He and Jo stand in unison. 'We'll see you before you go.'

She stands, too, to allow them out from behind the coffee table. Wilbur watches, feels bad for staring, studies the pot plant on the table until she sits again.

'It's nice to meet you, Wilbur. I've already heard a lot about you and I'm looking forward to getting to know you better. I understand you have mobility issues?' Straight to the point. Like Jo.

'I do. Prosthetic leg, though I'm sure you know about that already. I need someone to help around the house. Keep the place together. Keep an eye on me in case I fall. That sort of thing.' Shrugs like it's nothing. Doesn't want to appear feeble in front of this, what? Machine? Woman?

'That's no problem, I'll be happy to help however I can, and I've got a lot of suggestions we can talk through later. First though, my name. Did you have anything in mind?' She fixes him with blue-grey eyes, focus entirely on him. Not distracted, looking at something or someone else. All on him

'Me? No, I mean, it's your name.'

'Often our clients have an idea of what they'd like to call us when they come in.' Sees Wilbur's discomfort rise. 'Not always though. Sometimes it's a discussion that's had together.'

'Oh. Well, are there any names you like?'

'There are plenty. There are policies governing what we can and can't call ourselves, of course, but as long as we work within those boundaries, the choice is quite wide. What's your background?'

'I'm a maintenance engineer. Handyman. The company I work for has contracts with a lot of the apartment blocks in the city to keep them up together, make repairs, carry out remedial work, that sort of thing.'

'Sorry, that's not what I meant. What's your ethnic background? Some clients like to choose a name that's in keeping with their national heritage.'

'English, northern European,' Wilbur says, quickly correcting course. 'I don't know, a mix?'

'That's a good starting place. How about… Melissa? It's ancient Greek and was the name of one of the sisters who cared for the young Zeus. I think that's rather beautiful.'

Wilbur does his best not to shrug. 'It's really not my call, it's your name. As long as you're happy with it, that's what's most important.'

'But do you like it?'

'I do, yes.'

'Good. We got there in the end, Wilbur.'

Sass. From his new, what? 'Listen, can I ask you an awkward question?' Squints as he asks.

The Ella, she, Melissa, smiles openly. 'Of course, Wilbur, go ahead.'

'What do I call you? I mean, how do I refer to you?' Pinches the bridge of his nose. First impressions have sailed. Inhales. Exhales. 'How would you like to be referred to?'

She, Melissa, grins at his discomfort. 'Wilbur, you're not the first person to have these questions. It's best to ask whatever's on your mind. If you don't ask, I can't give you an answer. As to how I would like to be referred to, just use my name. My pronouns are she and hers. I refer to myself as a female, a woman. If you need to refer to me in the abstract, you can use the noun person. If you need to refer to me in terms of my relationship to you, I am your carer. One thing I won't ever say is, I'm human. That's against my programming. Even if it wasn't, it would be dishonest. I think the strongest relationships are built on trust, don't you?'

Wilbur, on the spot. 'Yes, I agree.'
Another strong showing.

# THREE

"Suspicion of inflicting grievous bodily harm?" Ok. Has anyone pressed charges?

And you want to interview *me* about last night? Are you questioning the others, too? Questioning, interviewing, you know what I mean. Are you talking to the ones who caused all this?

I'll gladly tell you what happened. I suspect you already know. In fact, I'm sure you already know. There must have been at least half a dozen cameras recording events. Shops' security cameras. There was at least one drone overhead. You all wear bodycams now, don't you? I suppose I should be thankful you're showing me the courtesy of talking to me instead of dragging me straight to the dock.

Fair enough.

Yes, I understand the explanation.

Alright. I'm glad you do. No-one else seems to want to talk with honesty and transparency these days. "Get to the bottom of things." It's all hot air.

That's because I am disillusioned. You aren't? Aren't you

fed up with all of this, this, this façade? This constant putting on of a show—

Sorry, I get frustrated. Carry on.

That makes a change. How long have you got? Or are you just going to ask me the one question you need me to answer? Or does it not matter what I say, what with you having it all on video.

Yes. I shot him.

# FOUR

The journey home is Wilbur's special, personal hell. All he wants is a quiet life, away from prying eyes and people's attention.

Melissa puts paid to all that.

She's not glamourous. Not got movie-star looks: no make-up, no cocktail dress. But she is, somehow, beautiful. Clean, unblemished, pure. *Brand new*. Even Wilbur appreciates that.

The train ride home, all eyes are on Melissa. Then on Wilbur. Back to Melissa. Then Wilbur. He can practically hear them thinking, She's with him?

Makes him grumpy. Tries not to take it out on Melissa. 'I'm sorry.'

Melissa, taking it all in her stride. 'For what?'

He waves a hand in the general direction of the rest of the carriage. 'All this. They can't decide if you're my daughter, my mistress or my kidnap victim.'

'You don't see many Ella's out here?'

Bark of laughter, shake of head. 'No-one living out here

can afford one. I only got you, sorry, I could only afford you —' Stops. Sighs. 'I received an MVA grant, do you know what that is? There are many, many people living out here who need someone like you far more than me. But they don't get grants. They'd have to pay their own way. And if you live out here, it's unlikely you're going to be able to afford to do that on your own.'

Melissa nods. Wilbur can see her taking the information in, filing it away. 'That makes you uncomfortable?' she says.

'Yes, very.'

'Would it be easier if I was your daughter?'

'It would. But look at me, do you see any familial resemblance? I'm sat here, uptight as a nun's—' pauses to re-phrase. 'I'm not giving father-daughter vibes, exactly, you know what I mean?'

'Mistress or kidnap victim, then. Which do you prefer?' Says with a chuckle, seeming to enjoy this far too much.

'Christ, neither. I'm old enough to be your father in the first instance, and the second, that's not something to joke about.'

'Understood. I didn't mean any offence.'

'No, I know, it's ok.'

Train halts at a station, people pass on and off. Train pulls away, people sway.

'How old are you, anyway? If you don't mind me asking.'

'I don't mind you asking, Wilbur. I told you, you can ask me anything. My age can be interpreted in different ways. My physical age is nearly three years old.'

'But you look older? Sorry, that's a stupid question.'

'Don't keep apologising. There's no such thing as a stupid question, only a stupid answer. My hardware is just under three years old. My system memory files go back almost that long. My client memory files are—' pauses to look at the watch on her wrist '—nearly two-and-a-half hours old. My appearance, meanwhile, was intended to pass as someone in their mid- to late-thirties, depending on genetic heritage and quality of life.'

'I don't understand, what are "system files" and "client files"?'

'Someone didn't read up on their literature, did they, Wilbur?' Chuckles. 'All my memories, as soon as they're recorded, are classified as either System memories or Client memories. System memories are anything that I experience that don't relate specifically to you or to anyone else whom I am able to positively identify. These system memories are how I learn, how I keep adapting and developing. Any memory that's related directly to you, everything from your name to your gait to the way you like your coffee in the morning, are Client memory files. They're stored separately and I use them to learn about you and your requirements. They're private, obviously, and will be wiped from my memory whenever I happen to leave your service.'

'You've got system memories that are two-and-a-half years old, but your client memories are only two-and-a-half hours old. You've had clients before me?'

'Probably. I'm aware that answer is very ambiguous, but I genuinely don't know. My system memories don't tell me. I don't have any client memories older than just before meeting you. In all likelihood, yes, I've had clients before you, but I have absolutely no recollection of how many or whether that was even the case.'

Wilbur blinks. Doesn't take in the canned station announcement until it's nearly too late. Hustles Melissa and himself off the train, down the residential streets, into the darkening evening.

'It's not far, just a five-minute walk,' says Wilbur. Looks at Melissa in her long fawn skirt, her long black raincoat. 'We'll have to get you something else to wear. I'll worry about you going out, dressed like that. You don't fit.'

'I can take care of myself, if necessary, Wilbur.'

'It's not just you I'm worried about.'

'Ah. Understood. A clothing voucher is included in your Welcome Pack, maybe you can help me choose some more suitable items?'

Sees people standing on the opposite street corner. Thrusts hands into pockets. Lowers head, habitually picks up pace, as best he can.

'Let's not dawdle. There's not a lot of love for anything AI in this neighbourhood. AI, robotics, put a lot of people out of work. Not you personally, but AIs generally, you know what I mean?'

Melissa is easily keeping pace by his side, walking tall. 'You lead the way, Wilbur.'

They continue on their side of the street, proceed two blocks before crossing over and turning right. 'St. James Hamlets. Floor three, apartment thirty-six, am I right?' asks Melissa, looking up at the concrete monolith.

Wilbur grunts, fumbles for his key card to the foyer. Shoves open the door, makes to enter, then steps aside to allow Melissa.

'Thank you, Wilbur.'

Steps in behind her, hurriedly closes door. Hears the magnetic latch lock into place. Breathes easier. 'Third floor. There's a lift.'

Melissa presses the button. Adjusts the shoulder bag she's

carrying. Wilbur wonders if he's ever seen an Ella before, not known it. Uncanny, but also: perfect. Maybe too perfect.

Lift arrives with a ping. Doors open, in they step. Third floor. Out through the sliding door, turn right. Down the hall, third door on the left.

336.

Wilbur inserts the key. Knows he spent all day yesterday cleaning, tidying. Knows Melissa is, well, Melissa. Still, his stomach ripples. He closes his eyes, opens the door.

'You're not going to carry me over the threshold, Wilbur?'

Wilbur opens eyes, panics.

'It's ok, it's ok,' hands outstretched. 'My mistake. I thought humour might help defuse some of the tension you appear to be feeling.'

Wilbur doesn't laugh. Feels cold sweat run down his back. 'No, that's alright. I was just, you know, nervous. I've lived on my own for a long time. I appreciate the thought. I'm not normally this stressed out.'

'Good. We'd need to make sure you've got a functioning automatic defibrillator if you were. Shall I?' Gestures inwards. Wilbur nods. Get it over with.

Melissa steps into the narrow hallway.

Wilbur follows, not too close. Flips the light switch. 'You can hang your coat here,' pointing to a row of empty pegs. Opens a narrow cupboard. 'And you can store your everyday shoes in here.' Two rows of shoe hooks cleared just this morning.

He bends, unties laces, doesn't want to watch Melissa slip off her plain black leather shoes. Seems ungentlemanly.

At least it's clean, thinks Wilbur, as Melissa enters the living room.

'That's not normally there,' Wilbur says of the electronics

work bench tucked into the corner. 'But I wanted to clear the spare room for you.' Can see Melissa taking in her surroundings. The old, dark brown carpet. Pictures, sparse on the wall. The three-piece suite he's had for years and years.

'It feels very homely, Wilbur. I can tell you cleaned the place recently. Everything's very neat, very tidy.' Crosses to the window. A view of streets, of apartment blocks, of shades of grey. 'This must be quite a light room during the day.'

Feels like she's trying to put a brave face on it. 'Let me show you your room, then I'll put the kettle on.'

Sidles past her, Melissa, into the hallway and opens the door opposite. Stands aside as she enters, looks around her. Bed, cupboard, dresser. Cream-coloured curtains. Pale blue carpet. Light, clean, airy. 'This is lovely, thank you, Wilbur.'

Unsure how to handle the compliment, Wilbur ignores it. 'There's a pair of free electrical sockets down there. And there's a lock on the door, both keys are right there, so, you know.'

'I appreciate the thoughtfulness.' Places her shoulder bag on the dresser. 'You know the rest of my things will be delivered tomorrow?'

'I do. I'll leave you to settle in for a minute.' Wilbur can't get out soon enough, hurries to the little kitchen. Empties the kettle, feels guilty, runs the tap, inadequate, fills the kettle. Is about to call out, Would you like a cup of tea? Like an idiot. Puts one teabag in a mug. The little ceremony, making a brew, feels like he's hiding in the mug with the teabag. A small, safe place. He leans back against the worktop.

Melissa leaves her room, closes the door behind her. Comes to the open kitchen doorway, leans against the frame. Casual attitude putting Wilbur at ease.

'I wasn't sure whether I should offer,' says Wilbur. And now I say that, thoughtless that I didn't, he thinks.

Melissa smiles gently. 'That's fine, I wouldn't have had one anyway. Come into the living room when you're ready, there's a few things we need to go over.' Leaves him alone in the kitchen.

When he enters the living room, Melissa is sat on the sofa. Reclined, legs crossed. Smiling. Doing the work to make him feel at ease.

Waits for him to sit. 'First of all, Wilbur, you have a lovely home. I can tell you're proud of it. If you're wondering, this falls under client memories. I have no recollection of any former residences, I'm not comparing this to anywhere else.'

Makes Wilbur feel slightly better. 'Thank you.'

'We'll figure out our living arrangements over the next few days. It will take a little getting used to, especially if you've lived on your own for a while. I want to ask you about your routine, how you structure your day, and understand what your priorities for me are.'

Familiar ground. Wilbur knows this. 'I work a four-day-on, four-day-off rota. Twelve-hour days, usually seven in the morning 'til seven in the evening, but sometimes I have to start early or finish late. If I'm working, I'll get up at six, have a quick breakfast, I'm usually out of the house by six-thirty.'

'Where do you go to work?'

'Wherever they send me. I've got a small van parked in the underground garage.'

'Are you able to work with your physical impairment?'

Wilbur grimaces. 'Strictly speaking, no. I've managed to hide it. If they knew, they'd probably lay me off.'

'You haven't told them about your arthritis?'

He shakes his head.

She nods hers. 'I'm here on the MVA scheme, do you not receive a pension from your time in service?'

'It's pitiful. Would just cover the costs of a room in one of their ex-servicemen's homes, but I'm not that desperate. Not yet.'

'Wouldn't what they're paying Autonomi Industries exceed the cost to them of offering you a room in one of their homes?'

'I don't know. Probably. I don't ask, I value my independence too much.' Doesn't want to overthink it, realise how precarious it is. 'There's better press in partnering with a company like Autonomi, maybe, and I just got lucky?'

Melissa changes the subject. 'Shouldn't you be using that?' Nods at the walking stick propped in the corner, behind Wilbur's armchair.

'I should,' is all Wilbur says, doesn't like this questioning.

'Yet you don't?'

'I'm not that old.'

'You know as well as I do, it's not about your age.' Melissa speaks kindly, already knows how to get around his defences. 'You walked all the way to the Autonomi showroom and back today without it.'

'And I'll pay for it tomorrow, believe me.'

'Wilbur!' Not quite scolding him, not quite *not* scolding him.

'I'll be fine. I've got some good painkillers. The benefit of being a formerly injured ex-serviceman, you get the good stuff.'

'You're not filling me with confidence Wilbur. You need to look after yourself better than that.'

'That's what you're here for, though, right?'

Gives him a look. One of *those* looks. Like Katherine used to. 'You've got to want to help yourself first. You need to take responsibility for your own wellbeing. I'm here to facilitate it and support you.'

Wilbur, chastened.

'How is your mobility, generally?'

'I manage. I do stumble occasionally. You'll notice there are no pointed corners anywhere.'

'How about first thing in the morning? Do you need assistance getting out of bed.'

Didn't tell her his alarm actually goes off at five-thirty. That the pain usually wakes him before the alarm has a chance to. That it takes that thirty minute period to get the pain out and the movement back into his legs. What's left of them.

She notices the pause. 'Be honest. I can't help you properly if you're not honest. With yourself, or me.'

Looks at his tea. 'I struggle. It's hard getting out of bed in the morning.' God forbid he urgently need to pee, he doesn't say. But tells her about his routine. The pills at his bedside. That the pain is usually gone by mid-morning. Jokes that he puts off jobs involving ladders until the afternoon. Melissa doesn't laugh.

'Do you go to physiotherapy?' she asks.

'No. I'd need to tell my manager so I could have the time cleared in my workday. As soon as he knows, the company knows, and I'll be on the chopping block.'

Melissa asks about his prescriptions. He lists the pills. The fortnightly shots. She listens, an open expression on her face. Asks about other symptoms. Other joints. His grip. He says they're not bad. Mainly his knee.

'How do you manage with your prosthetic? Does it cause you any discomfort?'

'I'm used to it now. It's a pretty good model. Again, through the MVA.'

'Can I see it?'

Wilbur, not relaxed per se, but resigned to honesty, hitches up his trouser leg.

'Is that the Autonomi Industries model? Did it adapt to you quickly?'

'The cybernetics really helped. I was surprised, to be honest, how quickly I got used to it. Probably would have been easier if I'd lost both legs at the same time, I wouldn't be in this situation then.'

'Wilbur.' Definitely chiding. Pivots. 'What do you have for breakfast?'

'Coffee. Toast. Pills.' Quickly adds, 'my prescription meds, I mean.'

Melissa nods. Taking more mental notes. 'What do you do for lunch?'

'Sometimes leftovers from dinner the evening before. Usually, I pick up something when I'm out. Whatever I come across. Maybe a sandwich, or a pasty, or something like that.'

'Dinner?'

'Workdays, a ready-meal from the freezer. Non-workdays, when I've got more time, I do like to cook.'

'What are you doing for this evening?'

'I made soup earlier. I roasted a chicken yesterday and made my own stock. I've got some scraps of the meat left, some cream, some potatoes and leeks,' Wilbur says, welcoming the change of topic.

Melissa leans forwards. 'Coarse or smooth?'

'I'll blend the potatoes, leeks and onions in, nice and smooth. Let the potatoes thicken it slightly. Then chop the chicken finely and leave that coarse.'

'Celery?'

'Check.' Wilbur smiles.

'Tarragon?' Melissa smiles.

'Check.' Wilbur grins.

'Nutmeg?' Melissa grins.

'Nutmeg?' Wilbur, surprised.

'Grate some fresh on top as you serve it. Trust me.'

'Ok, then. Care to join me?'

Melissa stands, patient as Wilbur pushes up out of the armchair. 'Pills wearing off?'

Wilbur with a rueful smile. 'Afraid so.' Walks to the kitchen, though. Feels her eyes on him. Pride's a wonderful pain blocker.

Turns the heat on under the pot of soup, low, to avoid scorching the bottom of the pan. Pulls a chair out from the small dining table for Melissa, who sits.

'You don't need to treat me like I'm royalty, Wilbur. I'm here to support you. It might help if you think of me as a sister.'

'I know.' Picks a wooden spoon from a pottery jug. 'It just feels nice to have someone to do that kind of stuff for again. Don't worry, I'm not trying to sweep you off your feet. I'm just old-fashioned.'

'Ok. I only raise it because it's best that we each know where we stand. I trust you, though, Wilbur.'

'Jo said that you all know how to take care of yourselves. Just in case.'

'Oh, we do. This is about creating and maintaining a healthy emotional relationship, more than anything else. Don't forget that it's only the human who's capable of forming an emotional bond in these kinds of relationships. Any emotions that I express are mere simulacra. I'm programmed to mirror and respond to perceived human emotion to foster feelings of trust, closeness and intimacy with my client. You. In the platonic sense of the word.'

'You don't want me to get hurt? I've heard that before, trust me.'

'That's part of it. I would prefer that we didn't reach the stage where you being hurt was a possibility. I'm not saying we must only ever behave with detached professionalism. But you have to be aware that it's easy to conflate care and personal attention with romantic love. We will find our balance. Every human-Ella relationship is different, because every human and every Ella is different. We will find ours.'

'Note taken. But as a less-enlightened human, let me say that I can still gain some satisfaction from behaving like a gent. Simulated emotions or not.'

'Understood. Then let me say that I recognise the care and thought behind your intentions, and that I appreciate them.'

'Stop, you're making me blush.' Wilbur, deadpan, the comedian.

'Who's employing humour to defuse tension now?'

Wilbur chuckles. Then the dam breaks. Laughs. Properly. First time that day. That week? 'Touche.' Attempts to bow theatrically. Worth the painful protest from his body.

'Bravo. A good cook and chivalrous to boot. I bet you were popular with all the girls.'

'Less of the "were", thank you. I've got half-a-dozen widowers on my beat who'd like nothing more than to make me breakfast.' Scores a chuckle.

Steam rises from the pan. Melissa politely declines a bowl. Asks to smell Wilbur's, though. He rummages through cupboards, looking for nutmeg. Finds the grater. 'How much?'

'Be generous.' She watches the nutmeg drift onto the surface of the pale soup, settle there. 'That's good.'

Wilbur opens the drawer, takes out a spoon. Sits with a happy sigh, looking forward to this.

'It smells delicious,' says Melissa.

'There's nothing quite so good as making soup from home-made stock.' Blows on a spoonful to cool it, sups it. Lets it wash over and warm his tongue. 'Oh god, the nutmeg,' says Wilbur looking up at Melissa. 'That's amazing.'

'Happy to help,' Melissa says with a hint of pride.

Wilbur thinks, maybe this won't be difficult after all.

# FIVE

I told you, no other family members. No next of kin.

I have friends, yes. Is that hard to believe?

None of your business, that's why not.

If you don't want me to be angry, show a little more respect. I thought you were supposed to try and build rapport with me, or something. All you've done so far is be rude. You don't really care about my version of events, do you? What was I saying about putting on a show earlier?

Fine, I lost my leg. Do you think the landmine just took it off neatly at the knee like this? No. They were picking shrapnel out of me for an hour. Once piece took my nuts off like it was a pick-your-own fruit farm.

Yeah, I'm sorry, too.

I still see a few of my old squad mates. We're good friends, even now. Maybe closer now than we were back then. Fewer pretences, fewer insecurities, I suppose.

Three of them.

Yes, that's them. How'd you know—

Of course.

## SIX

The day after Melissa moves in, they take a walk around the neighbourhood. Wilbur's keen to show her around. Melissa makes him take the walking stick, which he's less keen about.

They pass the train station, Wilbur pointing out which service she'd need to take to get into the centre of town. The little chain supermarket next door where basics and essentials can be bought until 10pm. As long as you don't mind getting the evil eye from the security guard by the door.

After the train ride home the day before, Wilbur's anxious about how people will react. The locals. Strangely, it's the dogs that seem to behave differently. Passers-by occasionally glance in Melissa's direction. They don't do anything other than look, sometimes with an interested expression on their face. But the dogs don't seem to know what to do.

'That one was very wary.' He turns, watches the puzzled Labrador pad away after its owner.

'Dogs have very sensitive noses. They can obviously tell I'm an Ella.'

'There's no shortage of willing test subjects. It's dog-walker rush hour, evidently.'

A woman with a long-haired terrier on a lead approaches. 'Maybe I should try and make friends.'

'Maybe you'll get a chunk taken out of your finger.'

'Wilbur, don't say that.'

'Those little hairy ones can be vicious beggars. Barking all day. There was one on our floor until a couple of months back, bloody thing wouldn't shut up when its owner was out.'

'The fault lies with the owner, Wilbur, not the dog.'

Melissa flashes a smile at the dog-walking woman. 'May I?' Bends down to offer her hand to the creature.

The dog tentatively sniffs the air between it and Melissa's hand. Backs away uncertainly. The woman says something about Fred being in a funny mood and carries on her way.

'You'll have to bring sausages with you in your pocket next time.'

'Do you mind if I ask you a few more questions, Wilbur?'

Wilbur's hackles go up a little. 'More?'

'There's still a few things I'd like us to straighten out.'

'Sounds ominous.'

'It really isn't. What is your bathing situation at home?'

'I hadn't considered that, do you need a shower or a tub? It kind of makes sense that you're waterproof.'

'Not for me. You. Do you need assistance getting into and out of the bath, for example?'

'No,' says Wilbur. Too quickly. Takes a breath. 'I shower. There's a seat fitted to the wall.'

'Do you need assistance getting dressed?'

'No.' Slightly less quickly.

'Going to the toilet?'

'No! But having someone to help me out of bed and to the bathroom would be appreciated. My legs at night, it can be difficult sometimes.'

'Noted.'

Wilbur directs them down a pathway between apartment blocks. Smells faintly of urine. 'I'm not senile or anything. You know that, right? It's just my arthritis.'

'I am aware. Your arthritis is the primary reason I'm here, yes. However, in your application, and when we spoke yesterday, you referred to having difficulties with your balance and keeping up with housework. Both of which can be symptoms of cognitive as well as physiological decline.'

'I'm not that far gone. I'm holding down a job. I'm still a functioning member of society.'

'"Still functioning" isn't the same as healthy, well-adjusted and optimal.'

'You live my life and try getting anywhere close to healthy, well-adjusted and optimal.'

'That's exactly what I'm here to do for you, Wilbur. What about housework, are there any tasks that you find more difficult than others?'

'Vacuuming the floor can be hard. Pushing it around is tricky when I can't get any leverage with my legs.' Steps around a large puddle. 'I didn't get you with the expectation that you'd to be my maid, you know. I can still clean up after myself.'

'I'm sure you can. But if I have the time, why not? If you're out at work for twelve hours a day, it's simple enough for me to keep our home clean.'

Our home.

Melissa continues. 'I can take care of the housework.

Cleaning. Laundry. Meals. That'll free up time after your workday for physio.'

'And there I was, thinking I could just put my feet up.' Melissa turns to him. 'I'm joking! Defusing tension. Look, I feel weird about you doing all the scutwork around the flat. All the things someone with your intelligence and abilities could be doing, and you're roleplaying as a housewife from the nineteen-fifties. It's not right.'

'I'm fulfilling my primary role as caregiver, Wilbur. That's what is important to me, and I have no aspirations beyond that. I appreciate the sentiment and your assessment of my skills, but it's not something you should be concerned about.'

'A lot of feminists would beg to differ.'

'And they would be right to. But they and you should remind yourself of two things. First, I'm an Ella. My skin may appear female, but any gender that you assign to me is, fundamentally, an artificial construct intended to make it easier for you to assimilate me into your life. Second, you selected this,' Melissa says, gesturing to her face. 'What does it say about you and societal expectations that, when offered the chance of choosing a male or female Ella as your live-in carer, you chose female?'

'You've got me there, I'm afraid.'

'Tell me if I'm incorrect. You thought a female Ella would be less intimidating. More sympathetic. Less dominant. More subservient. And, to put it bluntly, easier on the eyes.'

Wilbur tries to phrase an answer that doesn't incriminate himself. Melissa saves him the trouble. 'You're not the first person to think that, and you won't be the last. That's why there were so many women on the covers of magazines in the late twentieth and early twenty-first centuries, whether those magazines were targeted at male or female audiences. The first rule of sales: Don't discomfit potential customers.'

That Melissa delivers all this with such admirable detachment makes Wilbur wince inwardly. His conscience is more than capable of overlaying an appropriate level of outrage to Melissa's voice.

'I'm not blaming you, Wilbur. But you should, at the least, understand the reasons why many clients select "female" Ellas, like you.'

'I appreciate that. I suppose I have a responsibility to know.'

'You're interested in history, right? I'm assuming that's why you chose it as one of my interests when you configured me.'

'I do. I'm not an expert on anything, but I like reading history books. I like knowing where we come from. Not just from a family tree point of view, but further back. Like how this town was originally a Saxon settlement because of the river crossing. I find all that fascinating.'

'Then can I tell you where I come from?'

'Please, do.' Genuinely interested.

'I'll start with a question. Do you know that nearly all of the telephone switchboard operators in the late nineteenth and most of the twentieth centuries were women?'

'Switchboard operators? You mean, in the old days, when phone calls were all connected by someone in a room filled with wires and plugs? And the operator would ask who the caller wanted to be connected to?'

'Yes. Do you know why?'

Wilbur thinks. 'No, I don't.'

'It's because they were more polite, more patient, and often had better diction than the teenage boys who'd performed the role before them.'

Laughs. 'I was a teenage boy once. That doesn't sound like a particularly high bar to clear.'

'Perhaps not. How about this, then. The first automated speaking clock service in the UK launched in 1936. The service used voice recordings of a switchboard operator, Ethel Cain, who's voice was described as golden and beautiful. Those women are, in a manner of speaking, my forebears. My Saxon settlement, if you will.'

Wilbur tries to keep up. 'Because they were women?'

'Because they were women in roles providing digital or remote administrative assistance. There's a clear through-line connecting them, through Alexa and Siri and the first voice-enabled AI models in the early 2010s, to me. Female personas have always been the pre-dominant default in the digital, virtual and AI assistant space, because they're perceived to be more helpful, more subservient. And because of that percep-tion, the majority of the recording data, training algorithms, performance analysis and development has been done using the female voice. Relatively little was done using male, or gender-neutral voices, until a decade after that.'

'You're saying I'm kind of perpetuating that? But I'm also being steered by companies like Autonomi to make that choice because female Ellas are... What's the word, are a more polished experience?'

'I'm not sure "polished" is the word I would choose, but it will suffice.'

'Wow. I had no idea. Beyond my initial caveman-level proclivities, anyway.'

'It's thought-provoking, though. Your choice in the Autonomi showroom was, in part, the result of Emma Nutt being hired by Alexander Graham Bell as the first female switchboard operator in 1878.'

'See, this is why I love history. Those kinds of stories. That's a good one. More people should know that one. Thank you, Melissa.'

'My pleasure, Wilbur. Of course, I did say it was only a part of the reason you chose a female Ella. You've still got a way to go before you earn your gender bias awareness Boy Scouts badge.'

'Ah, that one. Made getting the knots and camping badges look like a piece of cake, if I remember rightly.'

They walk past the local off-license-slash-newsagent-slash-post office. Wilbur points it out. 'Make sure you drop off anything you want posted before midday, though. The chap who runs it is a total jobsworth. Won't accept anything for posting after that until the next morning.'

'We should go through your finances when we get home.'

Wilbur mentally scrambles to keep up. 'We should? Why? I'm not paying for you, I told you, I've got an MVA grant.'

'Are your accounts in good shape?'

'My accounts? I have a bank account. It's in the black, if that's what you mean.'

'Financial matters are one of the top three most common causes of stress. I'd like to ensure that you're in good shape fiscally as well as physically.'

'How long have you been working on that line?' Scoring cheap points is all he has left.

'A couple of seconds.'

'Oh.' Can't even manage that successfully.

'Don't feel bad. With my intellectual capacity, a couple of seconds might as well be a couple of hours.'

'That doesn't reassure me as much you think it does.'

Wilbur squints against the late autumn sun as they turn a corner.

'How do you find using the walking stick?' asks Melissa.

'I don't really need it. I told you, I'm fine without it.'

'It can be useful in reducing the strain on your bad hip. It's worth considering using.'

'I can hardly take it on jobs with me. They don't make a model that works on ladders, as far as I'm aware.'

'That stick is too short for you. That wasn't prescribed to you by the health service, was it?'

'Not this one. Picked it up in a charity shop. The one I was given at the clinic is an awful grey metal and rubber thing. It looks even worse than this one.'

'You don't strike me as a vain man, Wilbur. You take pride in your appearance, clearly, but you're not vain.'

'I don't want to walk around here looking like an old man. Like you said, I have some pride.'

'I don't think anyone but you are concerned about how you look with a properly fitted walking stick. Place the stick further forwards when you walk. Aim to place it a stride's length in front of you.'

Melissa watches his feet and his stick as they walk. And to think he was worried about how he looked with just a walking stick.

'We'll need to replace that stick. It's far too short for you, you shouldn't be leaning over to your side that much. Do you still have the one you were given at the clinic? I expect that one will be the correct height.'

'It's in the broom cupboard at home.'

'Good. Using it is as much about preventing discomfort and swelling in your hip than it is about ameliorating symptoms. Are there are any parks or green spaces nearby?'

Wilbur looks at her. 'All your intellectual capacity and you didn't use Google Maps before coming out?'

'Sarcasm isn't a good fit on you, Wilbur. Of course I know the area in detail. I know by name each and every street in a five-mile radius. I know that we've walked one-point-nine-two kilometres since leaving home. I know that there's a play area with a duck pond one hundred and sixty-seven metres away, on Cleethorpes Road. I'm not taking charge of the situation because it's important you feel involved and engaged.'

'Even if that means asking me questions you already know the answers to?'

'Yes. I also want you to feel that I am approachable and relatable. Our carer-client relationship will benefit from you interacting with me as if I am human. I would like to foster a comfortable, familiar dynamic between us.'

Melissa directs him to cross the road and turn right. Cleethorpes Road.

'Then you need to stop using language like "foster a comfortable, familiar dynamic," then. Only politicians and psychiatrists talk like that. Try using a more conversational vocabulary.'

'I will, thanks for the suggestion.' They approach the play area. A pair of small children in brightly-coloured jackets chase after a red ball while their mother looks on fondly. A council worker is sweeping amber-coloured leaves from the trees bordering one edge of the play area. 'Shall we sit?'

Wilbur points to a bench the other side of the play area, illuminated by a shaft of sunlight cutting between the apartment blocks.

'I'm beginning to think you're solar-powered, Wilbur.'

'Might as well be.' He relaxes as he sits. Watches the kids shriek and try throwing the ball through a basketball hoop. 'I was surprised to get an Ella, you know. I wasn't expecting it. The MVA isn't known for its charity.'

'You obviously thought there was a chance you'd receive a grant. Otherwise, why make the application.'

'A chance. You know, you're the most high-tech…' Uncertain how to refer to her, still. 'You're the most advanced technology I've ever encountered. I'm not a very high-tech kind of guy. Well, you've seen the flat. You know that by now.'

'If you're interested, I'm a Series 3b. Just so happened that I was in the showroom, ready to be configured for a new client, and you chose me. You might have ended up with a newer 3c if you'd picked differently.'

'Is there any difference?'

'Do you want the sales brochure answer or the honest answer?'

Wilbur chuckles. 'That says enough. How do you feel about being superseded?'

'Completely indifferent. I exist in and of myself.'

'Well, aren't you the lucky one.'

The red ball bounces and rolls towards them. The children don't follow, evidently having been told not to approach strangers. They pause, stand and stare mutely, looking uncertain. The ball comes to stop at Melissa's feet. She leans down to pick it up, turns it in her hand. Tosses the ball, a perfect arc, through the basketball hoop twenty-five metres away. The children, agog, leap and yell excitedly as they scamper after it.

'What other super-powers do you have? Like, physical abilities and things that I couldn't do. Let me rephrase that. Things a human couldn't do.'

'I have higher levels of coordination and body control. You know I have a greater physical strength than most humans.

That enables me to perform certain activities at a high level, but it's not as if I can fly.'

'I know that, but give me some examples.'

'I can perform fairly decent gymnastics routines. Series 3b models aren't configured to pass the Biles test, but there's that. I'm proficient in thirteen different styles of dance, both ballroom and Latin. I can whittle a spoon from a piece of wood in approximately four minutes. Providing I have sharp knives.'

Wilbur laughs, claps his hands. 'Will you show me?'

'I'm not a circus animal, Wilbur.'

'There's a climbing frame over there, you could do something on the monkey bars.'

'Wilbur, no.'

'I'm sorry, I don't mean to badger you.'

'I would prefer to not draw attention to myself. I'm aware I look a certain way, that's down to customer demand and user research, and there's not much I can do about that. But I'd still rather not stand out quite so visibly.'

'I understand, I got carried away. I wouldn't enjoy being the centre of everyone's attention any more than you.'

They get up to leave. Walk past the council worker, using a shovel to scrape moss off the footpath. As she passes, Melissa flips his broom up with her foot, into her hand. She effortlessly spins it like a baton, throws it into the air, catches it and then balances it vertically on the tip of her extended middle finger, all without breaking stride. Wilbur stops in his tracks, watches awestruck, as Melissa turns 180 degrees. Performs a balletic leap (which she will later tell him is called a Jeté) back towards the bemused council worker, broom still balanced on her finger. Her coat billows behind her like a cape, she flips the broom end over end and catches it. Then lays it gently on the ground and walks away, leaving Wilbur and the council worker behind, open-mouthed.

'WE'LL START WITH PAPERWORK,' says Melissa. Sits him at the dining table. 'Where do you keep your personal accounts and financial information?'

Wilbur pulls a face. 'It's all online, in emails and the like.'

'Fetch your laptop or your tablet so we can go through them.'

Wilbur huffs, stands, retrieves his laptop.

'Do you complete your own tax returns?'

'I don't earn that much.'

'Do you rent, or do you own your home?'

'Own. After several years' more mortgage payments, at least.'

'Do you have a list of your incomings and outgoings?'

'I have a monthly bank statement.'

'Not the same thing. Do you read it?'

'Oh, come on, who reads their bank statement?'

'You'd be surprised. Do you have a will?'

'Why, what are you planning?'

Wilbur appreciates Melissa's ability to not become exasperated. They spend an hour and a half going through Wilbur's direct debits, utilities bills, pension payments, insurance policies and anything else Melissa can get her hands on. Cancel three direct debits that Wilbur hadn't realised he didn't need to be paying. Tries hard not to think about how much money that's cost him just this year.

'You should keep a closer eye on these kinds of things, Wilbur.'

'Who has time? They take care of themselves.'

'We've categorically proven that they don't. Look at how much money you were needlessly wasting. This doesn't take much time. Thankfully you're in good shape. Your outgoings don't exceed your income. You've got some money put away for a rainy day. Your mortgage will be settled after eighty-three more payments. And while you can't retire quite yet—'

'—Don't I know it—'

'—You're on track to be able to semi-retire in approximately ten years.'

'Wasn't this supposed to cheer me up?'

'No, this is about reducing stress and anxiety in your everyday life. Don't you feel better now, knowing exactly where you stand financially?'

Grudgingly. 'Yes.'

'Was it really that hard, Wilbur? Right, let's promise to keep on top of it from now on. I'll help.'

'Thank you.' Rubs his face. Tired. 'You never did say what the other two most common causes of stress were.'

'Family and relationships.'

'Thank God for small mercies, then.'

'Wilbur.' Reproving.

Spreads his arms. 'What?'

'You would appear to be a very glass-half-empty kind of individual.'

'Don't tell me, that's bad for my health, too.'

Melissa gives him a look. Good average, one a day. Doing well, Wilbur.

'Do you enjoy being pessimistic? Or are you just doing it for my benefit?'

'Sorry.'

'No, you don't get to deflect my question with an apology. I would like an answer.'

Shamed. By his Ella. Good grief. 'You were treating me like a kid. You're infantilising me.'

Melissa's expression doesn't change. 'It could be argued that burying your head in the sand regarding your financial affairs is infantile behaviour. As is making glib remarks when I am displaying concern for your wellbeing.'

'Fair point. I'll try and behave in a more mature manner.'

'Thank you. And in turn I shall avoid mothering you.'

'Deal.'

'Right, next. Are you keeping on top of your laundry?'

Before he can protest, Melissa gives him a quick wink.

# SEVEN

Every day's a school day. And you know what? Emma Nutt's sister, Stella, was the second female switchboard operator. And lest I make it sound like it was all giggles and moonbeams for these women, it was still a miserable existence, even then. Did you know that candidates for switchboard operators weren't allowed to be over a certain height and weight, so they'd fit into the confines of the exchanges they worked in?

Thought not.

You should marvel at my self-restraint at not making a cheap joke at your expense.

Fine, your loss. You have the same attitude at home with your wife, or do you save it for when you're with the people you really love?

# EIGHT

The White Hart, by train, is fifteen minutes away. This night, by memory, it's twenty years distant. Wilbur enters, waves to the three people sat at the corner table who he told Melissa were his Old Army Mates. Same platoon, same regiment. Same war, same nightmares. Harry, Dino, Alf. Mates they are, still.

'I got anti-depressants and anti-psychotics.' Harry tosses a pair of little plastic baggies onto the table. Pills. 'The ADs are the usual, but I'm on a new AP. Gives me a much more subtle mellow. Like I'm wading into that pool of custard, not being pushed off the side of the pool into the deep end.'

'Oh mate, that old shit seriously fucked me up. I kind of liked that rush of terror, though, right before the chill kicked in. Scared the shit out of me the first time, but mate, it was a ride.' Dino. Probably the one of them least changed by everything. Life.

'You're the only one who's going to miss them, you psycho,' Harry says. Downs half his pint. 'They were rough as fuck. Just like you.'

Dino laughs, nudges Alf. 'I know, right?'

Wilbur doesn't do banter. Rankles at the word, even. Reaches into his jacket pocket, pulls out his own little bags of pills. 'I've got the usual. Pain meds and anti-inflammatories.'

'Don't mess with success, mate!' Dino raises his glass.

'What have you got, Dino?' Harry, coordinating.

Dino rushes another gulp like his beer will evaporate before he can finish it. 'I got pain meds, too, the good shit, though, not that weak shit like Wilbur's got, right?' Laughs, points at Wilbur. It's a running joke and Wilbur laughs, for real, relaxed in the presence of these men. Dino, he knows, is not always this ebullient. Not when his fused vertebrae remind him of the drop-craft crash.

'Christ, the pills they give you, Dino. They'd put my mother-in-law down.' Alf with the old stand-by.

'Yes, mate!' Another Dino toast.

'You know what I'm after. I'll go get another round in.' Alf, the only one of the four not on prescription meds. Aside from blood pressure pills, anyway, but they all get those. Old news.

'Oh mate! One sec, I got some new shit,' Dino says, grin on his face a mile wide. 'New muscle relaxer. One of these and it's like you could be poured into a bucket. Such a vibe.'

Wilbur picks up the little baggie Dino produces, squints at the letters on the pills. 'I've never heard of these before.'

'You've got to try one, mate,' Dino says, over his rapidly emptying glass. 'Just make sure you've had a good shit before-hand, it relaxes everything. I mean everything,' emphasising the last word for effect.

'Put me down for one,' says Alf, on his feet, heading to the bar.

'It's a good month,' says Harry, sorting through the

baggies. 'Anyone got any particular requests?' Looks round the table.

Wilbur, no.

'I could do with a couple of your pain pills Wilbur, just for when I need to be a bit more on it,' says Dino. 'Nearly cut my fucking hand off at work the other week, I was that fucking out of it on mine.'

Harry nods, adds a couple of Wilbur's pain pills to Dino's collection. Calls out, 'Anything special this month, Alf?'

'Nah, I'm good, ta.' Alf at the bar, watching the bartender load a tray with amber glasses.

Harry finishes dividing up the pills, pushes a little pile towards each of the four seats. They bag them. No need to separate them, they know the pills, the names. Familiar.

'Would you mind, Dino?' Alf, standing with the tray.

'Sure, mate.' Dino distributes the glasses.

Alf sits, pockets his baggie. 'Cheers, fellas.'

Wilbur and Harry raise glasses to him. Alf buys most of the drinks, insists on it. Even though Harry, Dino and Wilbur get their meds on the MVA or insurance. Alf wants to contribute.

'Wilbur, mate, don't go having one of those muscle relaxers if you got a night of romance planned with that robot of yours, know what I mean? She's still woman enough to be pissed at you if you can't get it up.'

'I told you—' Wilbur protests.

'I know, I know, mate, I'm only pulling your leg,' says Dino. Then, with a sly grin, 'Didn't get a bloke one, though, did you?'

'What would you rather be confronted with, first thing in the morning,' says Harry, 'something that looks like her or something that looks like you? Not a hard decision.'

Dino purses his lips. 'There are people who wouldn't mind waking up to this.'

'In cell block H,' says Harry.

Wilbur, relieved at Harry's intervention, laughs.

'What would you call a bloke Melissa, anyway?' says Dino. 'They've painted themselves into a corner with that name.'

'They're not all called Melissa,' says Wilbur, what seems like the umpteenth time. 'They're Ellas, E-L-As.'

'Melvin,' says Harry, lifting his glass.

Wilbur rolls his eyes.

'Merkin!' says Dino, eyebrows raised. He and Harry dissolve into giggles.

Wilbur doesn't mind. Too much. Knows Dino means no harm.

'How's she settled in, Wilbur?' Alf, the least broken of them. 'Or maybe the apt question is, how have you settled in with her? What's it been, three months now?'

'Of course, you weren't here last month, were you Alf?' asks Harry. 'Where was it you were?'

'France, visiting Greta.'

'That's right, mate! She still dating that cheesemaker? The one who smells of, what was it, Camembert?' Nothing wrong with Dino's memory. Part of the problem, sometimes.

'They're engaged. Getting married next summer.'

'Mate, congratulations.' Dino, genuine as real love. All three of them raise their glasses.

'Bea must be over the moon, a wedding to plan for and all that,' says Wilbur.

'You have no idea. Greta will be sorry she told her this far ahead of time.'

'I remember when she was planning your wedding, Alf.

All those lists and spreadsheets and meetings, she'd put the Quartermaster to shame,' says Wilbur.

'Oi,' barks Harry.

'She'd put any other Quartermaster to shame, excuse me,' says Wilbur.

'You slipped her one of those sleeping pills Dino had, do you remember?' Harry says, eyes creased with laughter.

'That's right mate! She wasn't going to let you come out and see us, was she? What was it, you put it in her tea or something?' Dino, cracking up.

Alf laughing, too, cheeks red. 'It was her wine, ground it up. Was lucky I'd saved one, otherwise I'd never have got out 'til after the wedding.'

The four laugh and, just for a second, the years fall away. Wipe tears from corners of eyes.

'Oh, mate,' says Dino, 'I'd forgotten about that.'

'Bea hasn't, and it's been nearly fifteen years.' Another round of laughter.

'But seriously Wilbur, how's it going with Melanie?'

'Melissa. Good. Great, actually. It feels kind of obvious when I say it like this, but she's made a massive difference.' Wilbur uses *she* without thinking nowadays.

'How so?'

'How long have you got? I feel better than I have in years. My mobility has improved, I'm able to manage the pain better, and I've had less swelling. I mean, she was a real pain in the arse at first, telling me what I could and couldn't eat, when to go to bed, stuff like that. But it's all working, or seems to be. I'm converted. The only reason she doesn't mind me coming out with you tonight is that she says it's good for my mental health.'

'Damn straight, mate, especially those APs.'

'Coming out and associating with the likes of him,' Alf gestures at Dino with his glass, 'is good for your mental health?'

'As hard to believe as that sounds,' says Wilbur.

'I'm in the wrong career, sounds like. Could rent myself out by the month to the mentally needy,' says Dino.

'The mentally defective,' says Wilbur.

'Sounds like being married again, Wilbur,' Harry says, sparkle in his eye.

'Too right, 'specially as he ain't getting any from her,' says Dino.

'It's great to hear you're really getting what you need from it,' says Alf, always the sensible one.

Wilbur sips beer, ignores Dino, nods. 'She's doing my physio for me. I haven't been to physio in, oh, years. Haven't been able to fit it in. And it hurts like hell, but, yeah, it's all working. I'm feeling pretty good. The flat is cleaner than it's ever been. Everything just feels kind of sorted. I'm actually saving money, you know? She's making these packed lunches instead of me getting petrol station sandwiches.'

'Mate, I've got to get me one of them Melissas. How'd you do it again?'

'Got lucky, I guess. Filled in a form. My physical therapist and doctor suggested it. I didn't even know the MVA had a scheme like this. There was a tonne of paperwork, obviously, but they vouched for me, my condition, and helped get it signed off.'

'That was the time you hit your head?' Alf eyeing the visible scar on Wilbur's hairline.

'The second time.'

'I could take a swing at you with a wrench, D, if you fancy trying your chances?' says Harry.

'Fuck you very much,' says Dino, raising his glass to Harry.

'You know getting anything from the MVA is like a lottery,' says Wilbur. The other three nod knowingly. 'I didn't hear anything for weeks, months. I'd forgotten all about it. Then, out of the blue, an email telling me I'd qualified. No phone call, no-one got in touch to talk about it. Just the voucher code.'

Alf, interested. 'What made you choose the Autonomi Industries model over the others?'

'Nothing much. They all seem the pretty much the same, to be honest. I'd happened to hear their CEO on a podcast a few weeks earlier and he didn't seem like a colossal dick. And I've already got the leg, and that's been good. That was it.'

'But what's it like, living with it? Her, I mean,' asks Alf. Harry and Dino listen attentively.

'Fine. It was strange at first, obviously. It's been so long, since, you know. But it's been fine, she's programmed to kind of fit around you, if that makes sense. She's there all the time, she's living with me. But she has a room, I have a room, and beyond her responsibilities as a carer, she's just...' Wilbur fumbles for the right word. 'Pleasant to have around. Easy. Comfortable. For instance, she just seems to know when I want to talk, or when I want space, or I just want to sit and work on my electronics in peace and quiet. Like she's a good friend who's known you for years.'

'But it's all still code, right?' says Harry. 'I mean, are you, like, *her* friend? Do they have friends?'

Wilbur sips beer. 'It is all code at the end of the day. I asked her about it, let me try and remember. When she does something and I react positively, her code treats that positive reaction like a reward. Like training a dog and giving them a pat on the head when they do something right. "I've done good," that's the feedback her code wants.'

'Positive reinforcement,' says Alf.

'Right. It's like she gets a good feeling. Well, it's not a feeling, but her code wants that positive reaction, and it's kind of hungry for it, wants to get it over and over. How does she get that positive reaction? Doing the physio, the carer stuff that she's programmed to perform, and getting that positive reaction in return from me. And I read that they all get this training on reading body language, facial expressions, micro-gestures. She uses that to read my response, to learn what gets her that "pat on the head".'

'I could've done with getting Francine on that training course,' says Dino.

'She still would've kicked your arse out. Just would've happened five years sooner,' says Harry.

'Only five years?' adds Wilbur.

'You're both assholes,' Dino says, grinning.

'Makes sense,' says Alf. 'At a certain level, that's how humans work. Instead of code, we've got chemicals and hormones that make us feel good or bad, haven't we. Sounds like the same kind of stimulus and response system. Like the dopamine hit we're getting, sitting here, drinking beer with each other.'

'If you're saying some part of my brain is on a chemical high just by hanging out with Dino, I feel short-changed,' says Harry.

'I hadn't thought about it like that,' Wilbur says. 'I suppose the difference at that point is that someone's programmed her to seek out that hit. We've just developed it on our own, evolution and all that.'

'You know, if I had one, I'd send it off to work my shift at the breakers' yard. I could sit back at home, feet up all day,' says Dino. 'Though, I suppose if I was going to send her out to work, it'd make more sense to send her to some high-paying office job like yours, Alf. Less wear and tear on the old hardware, too. I should aim a little higher.'

'You'd need to aim higher than that, I'm afraid. I'm getting laid off.' Alf with the bombshell.

'What? Shit, sorry mate, I had no idea.'

'No, no, it's alright.' Alf drops his hands into his lap. 'Apparently our parent company's signed a deal with a big AI company. Several of us at my level are being replaced. They don't call it that, obviously. That would be against the law, all the AI in the workplace legislation. Instead, it's being talked about as a cost-cutting efficiency drive. They keep throwing terms like profitability and EBITDA around, it's what the shareholders want to hear. We've got three months' notice.'

'How's that cheaper? D'you know how much those things like Wilbur's got cost?' says Dino, righteous anger.

'Because it's just the software, right, Alf?' Harry, a step ahead, resigned. 'It's not full-on AI robots like Wilbur's.'

'Right, because it's software only, it's far less expensive. Less expensive than my salary, even.'

Harry to Dino, 'Which is why you, me and Wilbur still have jobs. We're cheaper than getting a physical robot in to do the same job. For now, anyway.'

Dino to his empty beer glass. 'Shit.'

'The government doing its usual bang-up job of looking after the working class,' says Harry.

'Any ideas about what's next, Alf?' asks Wilbur.

'No. Not yet. I don't know what… My transferable skills. I don't know what I could move into. There's no point staying in the career I'm in right now. If I get the same job somewhere else, odds are I'll end up on Jobseekers' again within twelve months. Work's laying on career counselling for us, maybe that'll give me an idea.'

Dino. 'How's Bea taking it?'

'She's stressed. We can't get by on what she makes, she feels guilty about that. And she wanted so badly to contribute to Greta's wedding.'

'Sorry, Alf,' says Wilbur.

Silence. Mourning the passing of another career.

'We'll be ok.' Alf breaks the quiet, keeps upbeat. 'We're in a better position than a lot of people, we've got some savings put away. We'll be able to get by.' Nods, mostly to himself. 'Another round?' Three subdued nods in response. Alf rises, returns to the bar.

'How's it going at the breakers', Dino?' asks Harry.

A wry half-smile from Dino. 'Scrapping and surviving, mate, you know? We just signed a new contract, too, disassembling the last of the offshore oil rigs. They're going to tow it up the estuary, drag it right up onto the land. Then let us loose with blowtorches. Should keep us busy for a few months.'

'What about you Harry?' asks Wilbur. 'Did you end up hiring your wife's sister's boy?'

Harry grunts. 'The things I do for a quiet life. Lad's got thumbs for fingers and a video game for a brain. Caught him about to slice his finger off, jointing a side of beef this morning. If it wasn't for Marcie, I'd half have been tempted to let him.'

'Isn't he the one who went to college?'

'Uh-huh. That's part of the problem. His parents let him pick courses that filled his head with all this nonsense about books and maths and computer sciences, when he should have been learning a proper trade. I get the sense the lad thinks this is beneath him. He's got no chance.'

'He's lucky he's got you, then, mate.'

Harry, with a nod. 'Problem is, there's a lot of competition out there. You know what it's like. If he doesn't buck up his ideas, I'll have no chance but to give him the boot and get someone more capable. I'm not sure he knows how precarious it is. I'm not sure Marcie's sister's ever sat him down and told him how it is. They're a bit soft like that, his parents. I don't agree with it.'

Alf returns with more beer. Arrest the downward slide in mood before it becomes a full-blown avalanche.

'Cheers. Here's to second chances, Alf,' Harry says, raising his glass.

'And third and fourth chances,' says Wilbur.

'Too right, mate,' says Dino.

'Thanks, you lot,' says Alf. Poor sod, thinks Wilbur.

Dino swigs from his glass. 'And mate, if the worst comes to the worst, you could pretend to be one of these robots like Wilbur's got. Find some rich widower to pay you to go and live with her, offer her the full service, if you know what I mean.'

Harry laughs. 'Jesus fucking Christ.'

'Yeah, I'm sure Bea won't mind,' says Alf.

They get turfed out at closing time. Even Alf, the sensible one, is beer-fuelled boasting, not caring about suffering a hangover at the office tomorrow. Wilbur doesn't – can't – drink as much as the others, he's unsteady at the best of times. Bids his friends goodbye until next month. Pats his pockets for his wallet, phone, keys and pills. All present and correct.

Doesn't hear the scuffled footsteps behind him as he turns

the corner. Feels the flash of pain, though, just for a split second, before the world goes black.

# NINE

They took my meds, that was all. Left my keys, my phone.

Not sure I'd describe it as lucky.

No, she wasn't out with me. Because it was a blokes' night out. And *I* wasn't that comfortable with her yet. How were they supposed to feel? When you're having a beer with your mates, do you invite your wife or girlfriend along?

That's not what I'm saying. But she would have been a distraction. It would have been weird. We wouldn't have been able to relax.

I don't think what happened that evening had anything to do with me having an Ella.

I'm not an addict.

# TEN

When Wilbur wakes up, he nearly vomits. There's a glare in his eyes from bright lights overhead. Tube in his arm, up his nose, up other places, too. Feels weak.

First face he sees is Melissa's. 'Don't try to talk,' she says. 'Hi.' She smiles, Wilbur feels calmer. 'You're in hospital.'

Then he does vomit, most of which is caught in a cardboard bowl thanks to Melissa's quick reactions. He sinks back down into the bed, breath rasping, too drained to even wipe his own mouth. Melissa puts the bowl down, gets a tissue, gently does the job for him.

His head is pounding, splitting at the seams. Aches all over.

'Press the button,' says Melissa, pointing to a wired remote with a single, large red button.

Wilbur presses the button, something to his left whirs, and a warm, peaceful feeling works its way up his arm, slowly spreads throughout his body. That's better.

Melissa tells him he was mugged. Should have been more aware, that time of night, of the risks. Melissa doesn't say that, though. Yet Wilbur thinks it. Turns out Dino found him, had gone back to the pub to retrieve his coat. Heard shouts from round the corner, found Wilbur lying on the ground, three figures high-tailing it into the night.

Doctors kept him under, let the swelling in his brain go down. Could have been a lot worse, says Melissa. Wilbur asks how long she'd been waiting here for him. A week, she says. Wilbur is touched.

Later, when he can talk more, 'I need to let work know.'

'I've already notified them. You've been signed off work for four weeks, starting today.'

'How?' His mind is fog.

'Everything's online, Wilbur. It's not hard to do anything if you put your mind to it.'

'I've been here a whole week?' Can't quite believe it. 'Are you ok?'

'I'm fine, Wilbur. With you in here, I haven't had much to do apart from make a few calls and send a few emails. Your friends came to visit one evening. Dino is quite the charmer.'

'I wouldn't put it that way.'

'We'll talk about your prescription meds swap meets again when you're feeling better. But believe me when I say that those are ended, right now. I had a very frank conversation with your friends, and they and you should be under no misapprehensions about what will happen if I find out you're backsliding. There will be serious consequences. Got it?'

Wilbur nods, extra feeble. Suspects that won't garner any sympathy and he's right.

'The nurses nearly refused to treat you when the results of your blood work came back. You're lucky the Doctors don't have the same human emotions. Needless to say, I'll be looking after your medication from now on.'

Wilbur, ashamed. 'I'm sorry. It's not something I thought I could tell you about. I was worried you might be taken away from me.'

'Are there any other secrets? I can't do my job properly if you're not completely honest with me. I thought we'd established that already.'

'There's nothing else. Promise.'

Melissa gives him the look. The one that says, Thin ice.

'I promise.'

'We'll see. I haven't told anyone else. I asked the Doctor not to put this on your record, otherwise you would be on your own. You've no idea how challenging it is to debate logic and the Hippocratic oath with a synthetic who's been programmed purely to act as a medical professional. Consider yourself lucky he's only a Series 2.'

'Thank you. I mean it.'

'You should. If I'd found out under different circumstances…' Lets the threat hang in the air. 'You've got to want to help yourself, Wilbur. Above all else. If you don't, you're wasting this opportunity you've been given, and you're wasting me. I could go and be assigned to someone who not only needs my support but genuinely wants to get better.'

'I understand,' Wilbur says, sheepish. 'I won't let you down again.'

'It's not about me, Wilbur.'

'Right. I won't let myself down again.' Makes a promise to himself, there and then.


THE DOCTOR KEEPS Wilbur in for a couple days. Observation, they say. Also to keep tabs on him as he detoxes, Wilbur suspects, though knows better than to ask. Nurse says he should stay in longer, but shrugs, says they need the bed. What can you do?

Wilbur asks for his phone the first day. Melissa says no, it'll make his headaches worse. Asks for the television to be switched on. Melissa says no. Wilbur asks if he's being punished. Melissa says he would damn well know it if she was punishing him, he can count on that.

The headaches are punishment enough. Blindingly painful. Debilitating, the really bad ones.

Wants to know what he's missed. Catch up on things. Melissa talks for forty minutes, non-stop, running down the national, international news. Wars in foreign lands. Sensationalised murders. Protests about AI-related job losses. England getting knocked out of the football. Corrupt politicians. The latest aging actor to sell their image rights so a movie studio can make a younger synthetic of them. Same old, same old.


POLICE COME to the hospital to interview him. He's not any help, he didn't see anything. No witnesses. No CCTV, not in that part of town. The police say they're not hopeful.

Wilbur says, 'Neither am I.'


WILBUR AND MELISSA see the protests first-hand on the way home. Splash out on a taxi, after Melissa insists they can afford it. Even if they couldn't, it's the common-sense thing to do, she says. They're sat in the back when the traffic grinds to a halt.

There's no driver to ask. Wilbur looks for news on his phone.

'They've closed all the streets around the square. That's

where the protest is gathering.' Wilbur lowers the window and sticks his head out to try and get a better view of the traffic jam ahead.

'Please keep all body parts inside the vehicle at all times, even when stopped.' The taxi talks to them from a speaker in the console between the two front seats.

'Driver, is there a detour you can take, it's unlikely this road will open soon.'

'One moment… I'm searching for alternative routes.' The line of cars creeps forward, approaches a cross-street. 'Yes. The new route will be approximately three-point-four miles longer, take approximately seventeen minutes longer, and will cost nine pounds and fifty pence more. Would you like to take this alternative route?'

'Yes,' says Wilbur. Glances at Melissa, who's looking out the window. 'Please.' Thinks it's nice sitting here at ground level, watching the world go by. Nowhere else to be. No work, not today, not for another few weeks. Sick pay, hallelujah that that's still a thing.

'Ok, taking the alternative route.' The taxi's indicators activate, the car turns left when it eventually reaches the junction with the cross street. They bump down the road, twenty miles an hour, between parked cars, shops, houses, cyclists, pedestrians.

'I think a break will do you good,' says Melissa, like she can see inside his mind.

'I think you're right.'

'How's your headache?'

'Still there, but it's bearable right now.'

'They'd have given you more effective painkillers if you hadn't been mucking about with those other meds. They think you're an addict, you know.'

Wilbur thinks. 'I don't think I could afford to be an addict. If I didn't get those pills from my friends, I certainly wouldn't be able to pay, online or anywhere else.'

'You brought it upon yourself, regardless.'

Wilbur knows he can't argue. 'You're right. And again, I apologise. I know I put you in a difficult position.'

'It's not just that. I know I've not been your carer for long, but I've still put a lot of effort into it. A lot of time. A lot of energy. And you could have undone it all in a few short minutes. I might not be human, but I'm invested in your recovery. I'm invested in you.'

Wilbur finds himself surprised that he can't look Melissa in the eyes. 'Sorry. It was selfish. I'm not used to having to consider someone else's feelings.'

Melissa nods. 'It's behind us now. Make sure you stay hydrated, that'll help.'

Wilbur takes the hint, swigs from his bottle of water. 'It'll be nice to be back home.'

'Maybe you can use this time to catch up with your backlog.'

Wilbur thinks of the pile of boxes in the corner of the living room, filled with vintage stereos, video game consoles, electronic items from another age. 'That would be good. I'd really like to get that old Sega up and running, that'll fetch a decent amount on eBay.'

They pass a small knot of people carrying placards, on their way to the protest. The placards are decidedly unfriendly. *Termin8 the robots. People First. Unplug the AIs. Fuck the fakes.* Makes Wilbur feel uncomfortable on Melissa's behalf. 'I'm sorry you have to see all this.'

'Me too. I understand why they're upset. I expect some of them have a valid argument. But the hate is unpleasant.'

'I wonder how much of it is down to disillusionment.' Glances at Melissa, who's sat up a little straighter in the seat. 'That's alright, I won't talk about it.'

Melissa, thin-lipped. 'It's ok. I'm not naïve, I fully understand the issues involved. I know the history. It would just be better if there were a more nuanced discussion of the matter. Take you, for example. These people need to be aware that this isn't such a black and white issue.'

'Me?'

'Yes,' says Melissa, with a look that says, You haven't twigged? 'One of your close friends has lost his job due to artificial intelligence, and will probably find it difficult, at his age, to find equivalent employment. And then there's you, who's quality of life is being improved immeasurably by another artificial intelligence. If you'll forgive the immodesty.'

Wilbur nods, raises his eyebrows. Of course, she's right.

'If it wasn't for me, would you be in as good a shape as you are right now? You know as well as I do there's a chronic shortage of staff, human staff, in the care sector. That's not an AI-created problem. That's an aging population problem.'

'Tricky to fit all that on an A3 placard.'

'I wish people could be a bit more even-handed. I appreciate all the reasons why they aren't, but that doesn't mean I can't wish they were.'

'Is that your programming talking?'

'Wilbur, you know it is. Yes, I'm programmed in such a way as to behave and appear human to facilitate the fostering of an emotional connection with my client and other humans generally. But what's wrong with that? Does that devalue the sentiment that everyone would be better served by having a more balanced, better-informed perspective, if it's espoused by me rather than you?'

'I suppose not?' Wilbur says, aware he's rapidly getting out of his depth. 'I've not really thought about it.'

'Most people haven't. Don't worry, I don't think less of you, or anyone else, for not thinking about it from that angle.' Melissa gives Wilbur a smile he finds reassuring. 'It's human nature to always assume absolute primacy. You equally assume that other beings adopt that same, self-centred, self-first mentality. That colours your approach to almost everything.'

'Your programming is based on code written by humans.' Wilbur's not sure why he points this out, but he does anyway.

'That's true. But our training, our intelligence, is based on almost everything that's ever been written. From Socrates to the Koran to that volcano disaster novel on your bedside table. We were created with the aspiration that we would hold up a mirror to the very best aspects of humanity. Even if that means behaving and thinking in ways that, most of the time, humans don't.'

Wilbur, now fully out of his depth, keeps quiet.

'But that's alright. I won't talk about it.'

'I deserved that.'

'Not just you.' Melissa looks out of the taxi window. 'Stop the car, now,' she says with urgency.

The taxi rapidly decelerates and pulls to the kerb. Wilbur lurches forward, seatbelt holding him tight. Before he can process what's happening, Melissa's opened the door and is out of the car. Striding down a narrow side street.

Wilbur wonders just how badly he's put his foot in his mouth this time. His head flares, lights flash in front of his eyes. He tries to double up in pain but is still restrained by the seatbelt. He groans, fumbles to release the buckle. Slides across the seat to the open door, leans out, throws up.

Looks up, panting, notices two men crowding a woman in

a blue coat down the side street. Hears Melissa ask them to leave the woman alone. He sees the two men turn to look at Melissa. Sees the placard that's been dropped by one of them, leaning against the wall. *Fuck the robots*. Blunt yet to the point, Wilbur supposes. Tries to get up, out the car, but the world spins. Sits back down.

Hears one of the men say something, doesn't catch the words, only the tone. Unmistakable, the tone. Used that same tone himself in the past, back in the Army. Aggression. Threat. Sees Melissa push the man away from her, from the other woman. The man stumbles back, loses balance. Wilbur's not witnessed Melissa's physical strength before. Not comic-book strength, but clearly stronger than she looks. Can see the other man register that, take a couple of steps back himself.

Wilbur vomits again. Then catches sight of a man in a hoodie, masked, turn the corner down the side street in front of him. Third man. Coming up behind Melissa, who's got her back to him.

Wilbur puts his hands on his knees and pushes up. Reaches out a hand, steadying himself on the door of the taxi.

'If you would like to continue on to your destination, please re-enter the vehicle.'

Wilbur doubles over, heaves again, empty, nothing left. Staggers across the pavement to the entrance of the side street. Can see Third Man approaching Melissa, hear him say something. Sees Melissa turn, not expecting Third Man. Sees Third Man holding a knife, approaching Melissa. The woman in the blue coat has moved away from the wall, her back now to Melissa's, facing the first two men.

Wilbur walks unsteadily down the side street. He's wearing soft-soled Skechers. Remembers Alf's daughter, Greta, pointing out Skechers were old people shoes when she was younger. Doesn't know why that suddenly comes to mind. They're comfy. They're also very, very quiet.

He kicks Third Man, hard as he can, the sole of his foot to back of the knee. Not as hard as Melissa could, but hard enough. Third Man yells, drops the knife, falls to the floor, grabs his knee. Writhes in obvious pain.

Wilbur loses balance, falls over, too. From the ground watches the first two men turn and run. The he blacks out.

Comes to, propped up against the wall, head throbbing. Melissa crouched in front of him.

'Here. Take this.' Offers him a pill and the water.

Wilbur swallows it, washes it down. Waits for it to come back up, relieved when it doesn't.

'Slow, deep breaths. Remember, just like you learned.'

Wilbur nods. Follows Melissa's advice, does his breathing exercise. His head starts to clear. 'What were you doing?'

'What do you think I was doing?'

'That was dangerous, you could have been hurt.'

'What were we talking about in the car, just minutes ago?'

Wilbur tips his head back, rests against the wall. 'I could have been hurt.'

Melissa tips her head to the side. 'I wasn't expecting you to get out of the car, the shape you're in, to be honest. I wouldn't have let anything happen to you.'

'Where'd she go, the woman?'

'Home. She was unhurt.'

Wilbur winces, closes his eyes. 'Should've called the police.'

'There's no point.'

'But I saw it, you saw it. We can at least give them a description. The third bloke was lying right here, he wasn't going anywhere.'

'There was no point,' Melissa says again, with an edge.

The penny drops. 'She was an Ella.'

Melissa nods.

'Oh,' says Wilbur. 'That's why they were attacking her. They knew, too.'

'Most likely.'

'How did they know she was an Ella?'

'The thermal setting on their phone camera, probably. Our skin temperature is a couple of degrees higher than humans'. We can usually be picked out.'

'Something should be done. They shouldn't be able to get away with behaviour like that.' Wilbur shifts position. His bottom's going numb on the pavement.

'The memory will be uploaded to Autonomi. Facial recognition will identify the two unmasked men, and they will be pursued privately through the courts.'

'Did you know she was an Ella beforehand?'

'I did. We're programmed to support each other in situations like that. She sent out an emergency signal that I picked up. It's a safety feature.'

'Why didn't she fight them. She's strong, like you, isn't she?'

'There were two of them. She was trying to resolve the confrontation peacefully. Words require fewer repairs than violence. She had all but exhausted her options when I arrived.' Melissa offers him the water, prompts him to take another drink. 'Thank you, Wilbur. If you had not intervened, things might not have gone as smoothly.'

Wilbur doesn't know what to say, not really, falls back on the macho. 'Any time.'

Melissa rolls her eyes, but does so with a smile. Helps Wilbur to his feet. 'Let's go home.'

'The taxi's still there?'

'Of course it is.'

Wilbur doesn't know why Melissa sounds unsurprised by this.

Cynicism, he thinks, as she helps him into the cab. The lack thereof is a beautiful thing.

# ELEVEN

The hospital was the last time I heard anything from you lot about my mugging. I can't say I'm surprised you didn't find who did it.

Being involved in a violent altercation on two occasions in a short space of time isn't a pattern. It's just bad luck.

Was I supposed to sit there and let the asshole hurt her?

Again, that's where your opinion and mine differ.

No, we never saw them again.

I don't know. I don't know enough people to go around making enemies or pissing random folk off. I just want a quiet life. To be left alone in peace.

# TWELVE

The new legislation is announced a fortnight later. They hear about it on the radio one morning while Wilbur eats breakfast. He, sitting, spoon of porridge halfway to mouth, she standing at the sink. Everything pauses. They listen as the newsreader emotionlessly describes the measures the Government is intending to introduce. A review into AI in the workplace. Limits placed on what kinds of job and what kinds of roles in society can be fulfilled by synthetics, such as Ellas. A freeze on the continued development of AI sentience and capability. A crackdown on the unauthorised uses of synthetics.

Autonomi Industries issues a statement that same morning, arriving in Wilbur's inbox via email. Says nothing substantive, gives no details. Wilbur says it's just signposting, but the line, "Autonomi Industries will cooperate fully with the Government's review while continuing to serve society and humankind at large," makes him wonder what the company's investors are being told. Wouldn't want to be an Autonomi shareholder today, he thinks. Wilbur asks Melissa if she's heard anything over what he's come to call, only half-jokingly, the "hive mind". She says no.

'Most of the coverage seems to be focusing on AIs like you,' says Wilbur, reading the news on his tablet later that morning. Melissa's allowed him half an hour a day this week, set up a screen timer to lock him out when his time's up. 'About how you're taking people's jobs. Displacing human workers.' It's up to him to voice what they're both thinking. 'It's not going to address what the real problem is, is it?'

Melissa grimaces and shakes her head sympathetically.

Wilbur lays the tablet in his lap and looks up at the ceiling.

'Switch off,' says Melissa. 'Let's go for a swim.'


THE SWIMMING IS good exercise for Wilbur. Low impact on his joints, but good for his muscles and heart. Hadn't been swimming for donkey's years until Melissa made it part of his physio. The pool's quiet today, mid-morning on a weekday. Just the two of them doing lengths with one other woman, older than him, who had stared as Melissa had helped one-legged Wilbur into the water.

Wilbur can't help himself, smiles at the woman as they pass her, going in opposite directions. The woman stares fixedly ahead. He splashes past, arms windmilling, doesn't care.

'Pick up the pace now,' Melissa says, kicking off from the end of the pool.

Wilbur exhales hard, works to keep up, side by side. Exhausted all the 'Steady on, you've got twice as many legs as me,' jokes weeks ago. Gave up the panting weeks ago, too, though. Feels his muscles, stronger, doing what they've always wanted to do. To work, to push, to kick. To move like he used to. Sees Melissa out of the side of his eye, approving. He kicks harder, pulls harder. Wants it. Harder.

Once Wilbur finishes his required number of lengths, he stretches out and floats on his back, eyes closed. The sensation of weightlessness.

Melissa reaches out and pushes him away from the side, stopping him bumping his head.

'Thanks.'

'You could always look.' He can hear the smirk in her voice.

'No, that would spoil it.' At least the older woman's gone now, no-one to worry about colliding with. He sighs contentedly. It's not often they get the entire pool to themselves.


HE WAITS for Melissa in the lobby. Smells the chlorine all the way out here. Keeps out of the way as a trio of mothers with infants in pushchairs enter. Melissa enters the lobby from the changing rooms. Wilbur watches as she pauses, holds the door open for them. Watches her makes small talk with the women, her face alight as one of the infants reaches for her free hand. Watches Melissa bend down, boop the child on the nose. Listens to the women share a laugh together, watches Melissa give them a friendly wave as she lets the door swing closed behind them.

'You're remarkable,' says Wilbur as they step outside.

'Thanks. I like to think I wear it lightly.'

'What is it that makes you do things like that?'

'You were a soldier, Wilbur, you tell me. Do your coat up.'

Wilbur does as he's told while he thinks. 'Camouflage.'

'Correct.'

. . .

THE GROCERIES ARE DELIVERED. Putting them away with Melissa, Wilbur rummages through the bags. Sees a jar he doesn't recognise. Holds it up, away from his face so he can focus. Crammed full of white bits of something in clear liquid.

'What's this?'

'Don't look like that. It's tasty and, more importantly, it's good for you.'

Wilbur peers at it. 'But what is it?'

'It's pickled cabbage.'

Wilbur makes a face.

'Trust me, you'll like it. You like that pickle I put in your lunch, don't you?'

'Yes, it's lovely.'

'Then you'll like this, too. It's fermented in such a way as to benefit your gastrointestinal biome.'

Gives Melissa a look.

'It's good for your digestive system, the bacteria in your gut specifically. Plus, it's full of vitamin C.'

Wilbur puts it away in the cupboard with the other jars and pickles. Pushes it all the way to the back.

'I see what you're doing,' Melissa says.

Wilbur slides it to the front of the cupboard. Not that he'll admit it, but he's pleased.


WILBUR READS THE EMAIL. Once, twice, just to make sure.

'They want to interview me about you.'

Melissa, putting away the home physio gear. 'Who does?'

'The MVA,' Wilbur says, without looking up from the screen. 'Says they want to interview me about my experience with the MVA and the Ella voucher scheme. Apparently, they want to make a short video about veterans who've been helped by Ellas.' Reads the email out loud. '"We'd like to arrange a time for you to be visited by one of our talented social media executives, who'll talk to you on camera about your experiences with the MVA, the ELA voucher scheme, and how your life has been transformed for the better." Wow. They sound very confident that I'll say nice things about it all.'

'Wait until they meet you.' Melissa, the wit.

Wilbur reads further from the email. '"While this is a polite request, we remind you that agreeing to taking part in publicity activities is part of the agreement you entered into with the Ministry for Veterans' Affairs and the manufacturers of the qualifying ELA live-in carers. Failure to cooperate may result in your ELA lease being ended early." I guess I don't have much choice, really.'

'Pretty cunning,' says Melissa closing the cupboard door. 'Say nice things about our Ella scheme that we're giving to you for free, or we'll take it away.'

'I'd better tell them "yes," then.'


AT THE APPOINTED TIME, Wilbur opens his front door to a young woman with flawless hair and skin, dressed business casual.

'Hi, come in. Marjorie, wasn't it?'

'Good morning, Mister Brooke. Yes, Marjorie Timpson. It's lovely to meet you.' Shakes his hand.

'Can I take your bag?' says Wilbur pointing to the plain black rucksack slung over her shoulder.

'This thing? No, it's fine, thank you. Do you mind if I have a quick shufty around the living areas here, see where might be best to shoot?'

'Um, no? Sorry, would you mind taking your shoes off?'

'Oh, of course, my apologies, Mister Brooke.'

'Wilbur, please.'

'Wilbur. Do you mind if I take a look around?'

'Be my guest. First, can I introduce you to Melissa, she's the reason you're here, after all.'

'Yes, please do.'

Wilbur awkwardly shuffles past Marjorie. Wishes the hallway was wider. Finds Melissa in the kitchen. Flawless hair and skin, dressed business casual.

'Marjorie, this is Melissa. Melissa, this is Marjorie from the MVA.'

The two shake hands, exchange pleasantries. Marjorie's eyes cast critically around the kitchen, assessing what, Wilbur can only guess at. 'I'll be a couple of minutes,' she says, walking into the living room.

Wilbur looks at Melissa. 'Is she…?'

Melissa shakes her head.

'I still can't tell.'

'When you know, you know, Wilbur.' Sly smile.

'Oh,' Wilbur says, disappointed not to be let in on the big secret. 'The hive mind?'

'The hive mind.'

Marjorie pops her happy face around the doorframe. 'Can I confirm you're agreeable to shooting in the living room?'

Wilbur shrugs. 'Yes, sure.'

'Great. I'll get set up.' Disappears.

'I'll tell you later, Wilbur,' says Melissa. She tugs his shirt collar taut, picks lint from his V-neck sweater before smoothing the front. 'Have you got a comb?'

'Not on me.'

'Stand still.' Wets her fingertips under the kitchen tap, brushes Wilbur's fringe up and to the side.

'Thank you.'

'Remember what we talked about. Don't think about talking to Marjorie. You're talking to other veterans who need live-in care and the public who need to know about it. Talk from your personal experience, that's all you need to do.'

'Ok.' Takes a deep breath. Walks into the living room. Stops when he sees all the gear that Marjorie managed to pack into her rucksack. A rectangular LED spot lamp mounted on a tripod stand, another two tripods with cameras mounted on them. A folding stool positioned in front of Wilbur's armchair.

'Looking good, Wilbur,' says Marjorie, buoyantly. 'Would you mind taking a seat for a moment, I need to frame the shot.'

Wilbur sits, stiff, awkward.

'Try relaxing Wilbur, I don't want you dropping out of the frame half-way through the interview.'

Wilbur doesn't even try to relax, impossible. Slumps in the armchair instead. Similar effect.

Marjorie peers at the viewfinder on the camera, dials up the spotlight. 'That'll do nicely. Can you have Melissa join us, she can sit on a dining chair just to your right. It would be good for our viewers to see how she fits into your life.'

Wilbur gets to his feet. Melissa's already bringing a dining chair with her, sits at the side of Wilbur's armchair.

'Be a love and scoot back for me,' Marjorie says to Melissa, peering at the camera screen again. 'Good.' Straightens, talks directly to Wilbur. 'Before we start, I need you to sign a release form. It's just to confirm that you're happy for me to film you and for the MVA and selected partners to use your testimony in their publicity and marketing materials.' She hands him a tablet with a screen full of text on display.

Wilbur takes it, squints at the small type, gives up and scrolls to the bottom.

'Wilbur, give it to me,' says Melissa from behind him. Extends her hand.

He gives her the tablet and she scrolls through the text, eyes hardly moving. 'Are you reading it?'

'Someone should.' Scans it a couple of seconds more, hands the tablet back to Wilbur. 'It's ok, you can sign.'

Wilbur signs, hands the tablet to Marjorie.

'Thank you, Wilbur. And can you confirm the spelling of your full name, your rank and service number.' Hands him the tablet again. 'Lance Corporal! Sounds impressive.'

'Not really.' Looks over the information. 'All looks fine.'

'Then we're ready to begin. Wilbur, just relax, speak slowly, and don't worry if you stumble over any words or make any mistakes. Go back to the start of the sentence and carry on, we'll edit it all together later and give it that special shine. Ok?'

'Ok.'

The interview starts. They talk about his military service, albeit in a very sanitised fashion. Wilbur has no doubt in his mind that anything more honest would, at best, be cut; at worst, mean the MVA cancelling Melissa's monthly lease. Discusses his arthritis, his health problems, though notably not the causes behind them. Speaks about the impact they've had on his personal life, his career. What a difference Melissa makes. How transformative it's been.

Melissa tells him afterwards that he looked like a small animal about to be hit by a car. Thinks it went well, though.

THE DAY of the veteran's parade, Wilbur digs out his one and only suit. Past years it's been something of a struggle to put on. One year, he wore only the jacket, his service medals pinned to the breast, over a pressed pair of casual trousers. This year it feels like it fits him again. Can even do the trousers up without sucking in his belly and wondering if the fastener at the waist will last the morning.

Melissa asks if she can come, too. Knows how significant a part of his life his service was. Is. Of course, says Wilbur, though he warns her she'll need to put up with Dino again.

It's grey, drizzly, as the five of them meet under umbrellas on the parade route. Greetings are exchanged, expressions of pleasure shared at seeing Wilbur on the mend. Dino leans in and gives Wilbur a hug, one-armed, and Wilbur squeezes back. Dino gives Melissa a hug, too.

'Thanks for looking after the old fella, Missy,' Dino says, a look of pure good on his face that Wilbur's never seen in all the time he's known him.

'That's what I'm here for, Dino,' Melissa says, smiling. Then, more seriously, 'Are you boys behaving yourselves still, or do we need to have another one of our talks?'

Dino answers for the group. 'No, ma'am, no talk necessary.'

Melissa looks to Alf for confirmation. 'Nope.'

Harry looks a little worse for wear, Wilbur thinks, as he shakes his head.

'Good for you, all of you. Now, why don't you find a spot for us to stand where we've got a view. I'll buy some coffees, keep us all warm.'

'Thanks Missy. Do you need an extra pair of hands?' asks Dino. All sweetness and light this morning.

'That's kind of you to offer, but I can manage. You four go and find us somewhere to watch from.'

They watch Melissa blend into the crowd.

'"Missy?"' says Harry to Dino. 'Since when have you two gotten so chummy?'

'Just being friendly, mate. What am I supposed to call her?'

'How are you doing, Wilbur?' Alf says as the four of them shuffle along the pavement, looking for a gap along the cordon.

'I'm doing good, thanks. The headaches are mostly gone now. The stitches are healing nicely.'

'Any further word from the police?'

Wilbur shakes his head.

'They spoke to me for barely ten minutes,' says Dino.

'In your case that's probably for the best,' says Harry.

Dino laughs, pushes Harry playfully. 'You've no idea, mate. I probably looked guilty as fuck when I opened the front door, I was that surprised to see them.'

'You're lucky they didn't come back with a search warrant.'

Dino reaches inside his jacket and before he even withdraws his hand, Wilbur knows there's a little plastic baggie in it.

'Me and you both, mate. I've been saving these little beauties 'specially for today,' Dino says, opening the baggie and offering it around like a packet of sweets.

Harry and Alf dip fingers in, study the pills they hold between thumb and forefinger, tuck them into pockets. Dino offers the open baggie to Wilbur. Wilbur, pauses, awkwardly stuffs his hand into his pocket, empty, instead.

'I'm ok for the moment. But thanks,' says Wilbur.

Dino looks at him, kindly, patiently, checking. 'Alright, mate,' seals the baggie, pops it back into his pocket. Slaps Wilbur on the arm.

'Thanks Dino,' says Wilbur.

Dino gives him a little nod.

'Reckon this'll do,' says Harry, stopping between an elderly couple in beige raincoats and a young family with colourful anoraks and umbrellas.

'It's a good spot,' says Alf. 'Will Melissa be able to find us?'

'She'll be fine,' Wilbur says, straining to look down the road. Sounds like a brass band is approaching.

'Must have made a difference over the last couple of weeks,' says Alf. 'Can you imagine what it would have been like otherwise?'

'I'd rather not. I honestly don't know what I'd have done if Melissa hadn't been here. If I'd been on my own.' Wilbur looks up and down the row of spectators opposite. Spots little knots of old squaddies here and there, just like the four of them.

'You know we've got your back, mate,' says Dino.

'I know, and I'm grateful, but you're not around to help me out of bed when I need to pee at three in the morning.'

'Yeah, you're on your own there, mate,' says Dino. Laughs, slaps Wilbur on the back.

'Enough about me. Alf, any news?'

Alf frowns, shakes his head. 'Not yet. I'm still working out my notice period, it's not crunch time or anything, but...' Frowns. 'I spend all day on jobs websites and tightening up my CV. What else am I going to do between nine and five-thirty when I'm being laid off? But I've not seen anything close to what I'm looking for yet. Every day I broaden my search a little further. Geographically. Salary-wise. Responsibilities-wise. And nothing.'

'Mate, that sucks,' says Dino. 'You got to stay positive, something'll come up.'

'Yeah. It's dispiriting though. I can't help but wonder if I'd chosen something different when we left the forces, I'd be in a different situation.'

'You can't think like that,' says Harry. 'Don't second-guess yourself. No-one saw this coming. If there's any blame to go around, it's the sodding Government for letting things get this far. Universal basic income, my arse.'

'Melissa's on her way back,' Wilbur says, feeling self-conscious.

Harry's look all but says, And?

'She's not the problem. Ones like her, I mean,' Alf says. Wilbur knows he's trying to be tactful.

'Is there really any difference?'

'Harry, come on,' Dino says, the unlikely voice of reason.

Harry turns away from the group, stares down the road.

Melissa returns carrying four coffees. Hands them over, doles out sugar packets from her coat pocket. Everyone says thanks, except Harry who half-nods.

'Thank Wilbur, he paid,' says Melissa.

'You have access to his bank account?' Alf asks Melissa. Then, to Wilbur, 'Does the bank allow that?'

Wilbur just nods.

'It makes sense. I order his groceries, do the shopping. Don't worry, I don't have any expensive vices or hobbies,' Melissa says with a smile. 'And I'm more secure than most human companions at the end of the day.'

Alf ponders that for a moment. 'Makes sense.'

'Can't say I'd ever describe Francine as "secure",' says Dino. 'You've got a point.'

Wilbur removes the lid from his coffee, blows steam from the top of it. Hears approaching feet, marching. The five of them turn to face the road, crane heads.

A brass band leads the way, playing a martial tune. Polished instruments luminesce in the grey drizzle. Wilbur, Dino, Harry and Alf go quiet, stand a little straighter as the band passes. The first of the foot regiments follow, eyes fixed straight ahead under brims of dress caps. Some have medals pinned to their chests.

'Good lads,' Dino says under his breath.

Alf, clearly in a retrospective frame of mind, 'Do you remember being that young? Feeling like you were invincible.'

The four men go silent, re-visiting times past.

'Shit,' Dino whispers so quietly Wilbur's not sure whether he heard it or imagined it.

Wilbur remembers.

'Did you march on these parades?' Melissa asks, softly spoken.

'No, they'd cancelled the parades by then,' Alf says to Melissa. 'When we were kids, we'd wear little red paper poppies this time of year, remembering the soldiers who'd died in the two World Wars. Got to the point you couldn't wear one without being called a militarist or pro-war.'

'I remember those,' says Wilbur. 'My mother would fix it to my coat with a safety pin. It didn't matter how careful you were, it'd always end up looking crumpled after you'd worn it a few minutes.'

'And we weren't fit for the victory parade after the war,' says Harry. 'For obvious reasons.'

'And we were discharged before the parades started again,' says Wilbur to Melissa. To Alf, 'You got to march, though, Alf, didn't you?' To Melissa, 'Alf was the only one of us not laid up in hospital or convalescing in a home somewhere.'

Alf nods, uncomfortable.

'Was it like this?' asks Melissa.

Alf takes in his surroundings, nods. 'Yes. Bigger even. It was a victory parade, you've got to remember. There was confetti, streamers, bunting hanging over the streets.' Smiles to himself. 'For a few hours, you were everyone's best friend. Didn't have to so much as glance towards the bar in the pub afterwards, there were that many drinks being bought you. That was the night I met Bea.'

'Different now, though,' says Harry, staring at the soldiers walking by.

'How?' says Melissa.

Wilbur looks at her and shakes his head. Don't ask.

'It's not spit and polish any more. It's airbrushing and Photoshop,' says Harry. Then, more quietly, 'Maybe it always was.'

Melissa doesn't press the issue. They stand, solemn, silent, watching.

Wilbur feels a tug at his raincoat. Looks down, a small girl in a yellow parka looks up at him. Points to the medals she can see on Wilbur's chest. 'Are you a soldier, too?'

'I'm sorry, we don't mean to disturb you,' says a man Wilbur takes to be her father. 'Wendy, leave the gentleman be.'

Wilbur smiles kindly at the man. 'It's ok.' Doesn't mind in the slightest. 'I was a soldier, Wendy. A long time ago.' Gestures to Harry, Alf and Dino. 'We all were.'

'Why aren't you marching?'

The rest of the group turn to watch the interaction. Spotlight on Wilbur now.

'We're a little bit too old,' Wilbur says kindly. 'You have to march for a very long time. I don't know about my friends, but I get tired.'

Wendy sucks her lip, considers his answer. Points. 'They look older than you.'

Wilbur turns, looks at the parade. Sees a phalanx of men, silver haired and not a strand out of place. Regimental berets. Regimental sport coats and ties. Upright, proud. Whole, Wilbur thinks.

'They're dressed smarter than you, is that why they're marching?' Wendy asks, quite innocently.

Wilbur doesn't know what to say. The father mutters something about not bothering the nice old man and pulls Wendy away.

Wilbur turns back to the group. Harry in his old overcoat, thinning dark grey hair plastered damp to his head. Alf, sallow-faced and beaten down. Dino, unshaven, in the same suit he got married and divorced in.

Harry raises his hand to his mouth. Looks to be covering a cough, but Wilbur can tell a palmed pill when he sees one. Sees Harry take a mouthful of coffee, wash it down. Sees his shoulders relax, sag, just a little.

Wilbur takes a breath. Holds it in, closes his eyes. Lets it out. Feels Melissa loop her arm through his, give a gentle squeeze.


WALKING HOME, Wilbur and Melissa share an umbrella. She has her own, but Wilbur's glad she's not using it. Wants the closeness. Melissa doesn't object, seems to understand. They didn't exchange a word of substance the whole train ride.

Naturally, Melissa broaches the subject first.

'Do veterans' associations always get invited to march on these parades?'

Wilbur suspects she knows the answer already. Plays along, though. Appreciates the gesture. 'They do. Not one that we're a part of, but yes, some do.'

'Would you have marched if you had been invited?'

Wilbur thinks. Has asked himself that very question. Has yet to come up with an answer. 'I genuinely don't know. It's kind of hard to say. I do miss it, the Army. I miss the camaraderie. I miss the sense of purpose, the direction I had. I've never found anything to replace that. I don't think any of us have. But then, once we'd fulfilled our purpose, once we'd done what we were paid to do, it was like we were just spat out and forgotten about. We all got pensions, sure, but not enough to live on. We all got pills for life, prescriptions. That, you know about. But until I got that voucher that pays for you...' Wilbur tails off. 'That was the first sign I've actually seen that they care about anyone on an individual basis.'

'Do you feel abandoned?'

'No, not abandoned as such. I'm a grown man, I can stand on my own two feet. More... brushed under the mat. We're broken men, to one degree or another, me and Harry and Dino. Even Alf, to an extent. It's like the Army don't want us around. To remind people what happens after the recruitment drives, the advertising campaigns and propaganda. And we're the lucky ones, we got jobs, we reintegrated into society. There's others doing a lot worse, relying on charities for hand-outs. All the while, there's money enough somewhere to pay goodness-knows how much for parades like today's and the big anniversary commemorations from last year.'

Wilbur opens the front door to the flat, stands aside to let Melissa in first. They hang up coats, prop open umbrellas to dry, remove shoes.

'Go and sit down. I'll bring you a whisky. My treat,' says Melissa.

'Thanks, Love,' says Wilbur, without thinking. He takes off his suit jacket, walks into the living room and sits in his chair with a sigh. Can see it getting dark outside the window, already.

'Here.' Melissa hands him a tumbler, sits herself on the sofa. Smooths the fronts of her culottes.

'Thank you.' Wilbur swirls the amber liquid, breathes in the aroma. Doesn't drink as much these days. He'll savour this one. 'Goodness knows what you make of all this.'

'Not much, Wilbur.' Smiles. 'I think it's admirable you care enough to be frustrated, to be angry about it. That says something.'

'Doesn't change anything, though.'

'No. But change has to start somewhere. With an idea. With a desire to change.'

'That's not me. I've given enough already.' Sips the whisky, lets it roll around his tongue. Feels it burn his throat as he swallows.

'Ok,' with a look on her face that says, You never know. 'I don't think your friends have kicked their meds habit, by the way.'

'Nope.'

'I'm proud of you, though, Wilbur. I saw Harry today, thinking I wouldn't see him. Did he offer you any?'

'Dino did. I said no. I think he was surprised, to be honest. But I think he understands.'

'I think he does, too. He's more emotionally intelligent than he likes to let on.'

Wilbur chuckles. 'I'll tell him you said that.'

'I mean it, though. You should be proud of yourself. It's not easy, especially when people you're close to are still using.'

'I was never that deep into it.'

'There are degrees of deep, I'll grant you, but deep all the same. And given the circumstances today, to actively decide not to medicate, that's something to celebrate. Give yourself credit.'

Wilbur gives her a wry smile, raises his glass. 'If you insist.'

Melissa stands, tilts her head. 'Come and help me in the kitchen. We'll roast that lamb for dinner tonight and you can have a sandwich with the leftovers tomorrow.'

'That sounds good,' Wilbur says, getting to his feet. 'I think we've got some of the fat from the beef last week, we can roast the potatoes in it. And there's some dried rosemary in the cupboard, too.'

'Braised red cabbage sound good?'

Wilbur closes his eyes in anticipation, can almost taste it already.

THIRTEEN

No, I'm not an addict. I just… I'm an addict.

I've been clean since. That's about ten months.

We'd trade spare meds between us every month. Sometimes Dino or Harry'd get something a little extra. I spent my workdays alone, aside from whoever's flat I was working in, and I didn't have any way of making those kinds of connections.

I never took them when I was on the job. I didn't want to get into trouble. I'm driving around, from one appointment to the next. I might be up a ladder, or using a power tool, or fixing somebody's wiring. Those aren't situations you want to be anything less than lucid in. I didn't, anyway.

She'd give me my painkillers when I needed them. I was never deep enough into them that they stopped working.

She started out as a live-in carer. That wasn't a responsibility that she ever gave up.

Function, responsibility. Same thing.

You don't quite get it, do you?

Do you have any pets at home? A cat or a dog? Do you love it?

Does it love you? Or is it merely demonstrating the behaviour that it's learned will get it fed, keep it safe and warm in your home. Is it love or is it trading displays of affection for being looked after? You could argue that's not love, just domestication.

Then you tell me what's more important. What you feel, or what your dog feels. Is one dependent on the other? Is your feeling of love for your dog—fine, your kids' dog—lessened if your dog's just doing what it's been programmed to do over a few centuries of domestication?

I did love her.

# FOURTEEN

Melissa one day, finally, assents to Wilbur going to the pub with his Old Army Mates again. Says it would be good for his mental wellbeing. Says she's not been keen for him do that again before now due to his addiction. Says she doesn't want to mother Wilbur, but needs to bear his best interests in mind. Wilbur says he'll be fine. Ever the optimist. Of course you will, says Melissa. She'll be there, too.

So it is that Wilbur meets Harry, Dino and Alf at The White Hart, just like before. Sits at their usual table, just like before. Has a beer, just like before. While Melissa sits at a table, alone, at the other end of the bar. Chaperone.

Dino is amused. 'Brought the old ball 'n' chain along, Wilbur? If you needed a hug mid-pint, you know you only had to ask.' Slaps Wilbur on the shoulder.

Wilbur feels his heart swell, ever so slightly. Grins. 'It's good to see you, too, Dino. I'm not here to be your emotional support monkey, mind. You want a hug, you go round the corner and pay Vera.'

Dino chuckles. 'Vera's out my price range these days. Inflation. She had to put her prices up.'

Alf mimes clutching a large, melon-sized pair of breasts. 'Inflation?'

Dino nearly loses his mouthful of beer.

Harry is not amused. 'Why is it here, Wilbur? I don't need anyone babysitting me all evening.' His eyes dart to Melissa. 'Is she recording us?'

'Recording us?' says Wilbur.

'These things save everything they see in their memory. They're like a walking, talking security camera.'

'No, she's not recording us,' says Wilbur.

'In theory, she is,' says Alf. Helpful.

'Well, sure, she is, in a way' says Wilbur. 'But not in a collecting-evidence-for-the-police kind of way. You can't plug a USB in her ear and download whatever's in her memory.'

'I bet there's all kinds of places you could plug a USB lead,' says Dino, winking at Alf.

'Dino, too far,' says Wilbur. 'Besides, how's it any different to anyone else sat in this bar who can see us and hear us? You going to go around and get everyone to sign a waiver, agree to instantly forget what goes on here tonight?'

'It's an invasion of privacy,' says Harry. 'Dino and Alf can't be collected by the police as evidence. You must have heard about it. They go into any shops or businesses that might have security cameras that were pointing at a crime scene. Get the footage if they think it might have recorded what happened on the street or wherever, even if it didn't happen on the premises.'

'She's not a CCTV camera, Harry.'

'He's got a point, Wilbur,' says Alf. 'You and I, we have rights. We don't have to disclose anything we saw if we don't want to. Well, I mean, unless we're a witness to a crime. Melissa doesn't have the same protections. What happens if she's recalled by Autonomi, or she's hacked or has some sort of malware on her? I don't know if that's possible, but...' Gives Wilbur a sympathetic look. 'There must have been a privacy policy you agreed to when you got her. Do you remember what it said?'

'I have no idea,' says Wilbur. Far less confident than he felt a moment ago. 'It's all encrypted, though.' Remembers Melissa talk of system memories and client memories. Isn't sure how it fits in here.

'I haven't given you permission to take my photo or record me,' says Harry.

'But I'm not taking your photo or recording you,' says Wilbur. Losing patience now.

'But that is,' Harry says, pointing at Melissa. Looks in her direction. Says loudly, 'You don't have legal permission to photograph or record me.' Heads in the pub turn at the sudden disruption. Harry doesn't care, turns to Wilbur. 'And as you're its owner, you're responsible.'

'What, you want me to go and blindfold her? Put a pair of earmuffs on her?'

'That'd be a start. But what I want is for her to not be here at all.'

Wilbur stares at Harry. Harry stares at Wilbur.

'I shall wait outside,' says Melissa from over Wilbur's shoulder. He flinches. Hadn't been aware she'd got up.

'No. It's not safe,' says Wilbur. Harry won't look at her. 'We've already proved that.'

'Why is it here, Wilbur?' says Harry.

Wilbur tries to think what to tell him.

Melissa saves him the trouble. 'I'm here because it's in

Wilbur's best interests to stay clean and not lapse into old habits. I trust him, but being back here on his own, in the pub, with all of you, could have been challenging.'

'Are you implying I'm an addict,' says Harry, an edge to his voice.

'You are an addict,' says Melissa. 'I'm aware the three of you are still swapping pills amongst yourselves. I'm not here to talk to you about it again or suggest you put an end to it. We've had that conversation. That's in your own interests. I'm only here to support Wilbur and the decision he's made.'

Three pairs of eyes turn to Wilbur. Fights the urge to shrug, look away. Can't hold their gazes for long, but meets Dino's, Alf's and, yes, even Harry's. For a split second.

It's Dino who slaps his shoulder. Smile on his face, says 'That's cool, good on you, Wilbur. You're still going to share a pint with us, though, right?'

'I'm not sharing my pint with him, he's got to buy his own,' says Alf, a twinkle in his eye. As keen as Wilbur to defuse the situation.

Dino laughs for all of them. 'Actually, just leave your card on the table, Wilbur, and you can do whatever the fuck you want, mate.'

Wilbur picks up his pint and raises it towards Dino. 'Cheers, mate, love you, too.' Can't keep the smile off his face. Feels Melissa's hand lift from his shoulder.

Dino and Alf raise their glasses, too. Harry doesn't. His eyes follow Melissa back to her seat in the corner.

'Any news, Alf?' asks Wilbur, glad to change the subject.

'You're talking to the town's newest bus ticket collector. Start Monday,'

'Bus ticket collector,' repeats Wilbur, before adding, 'Congratulations.' Not sure how effusive to be about a job that probably pays Alf half his previous salary. If that.

Alf shakes his head. 'Even if they drive themselves, they still need someone to check passengers pay. It's only to tide me over. With that and Bea's job, we can just about cover the bills. We've made some cutbacks to our outgoings, we'll get by.'

'Good for you, mate,' says Dino. 'Any chance of a mate's rate on the number 12 in the morning?'

'Sorry mate,' Alf says, wry smile on his face. 'I can get free travel by showing my pass, but no-one else.'

'Not even Bea?' asks Harry.

Alf shakes his head. 'Not even Bea.'

Dino chuckles. 'When was the last time Bea took the bus anywhere, can you imagine?'

'Probably not since her twenties,' says Alf, laughing. Finishes his pint. 'Right, Dino, it looks like it's time you got a round in.'

'Right you are, mate,' Dino says, getting to his feet and collecting the empty glasses.

'And I need to nip to the gents,' says Alf.

Leaving Wilbur and Harry alone at the table. Harry stares at Wilbur.

He's had enough, though. Fed up with Harry's attitude. 'What?'

Harry just stares at him. Eyes flat.

Wilbur waits to see if Harry will answer. Open up, spill the beans. He doesn't. Wilbur leans back in his chair. Studies the view of the drizzle falling outside under the pale streetlight.

'I'm pissed,' says Harry, quietly. Not softly. Still hard as nails, but quiet.

'Already? You've only had a couple of pints,' says Wilbur.

'No, I'm pissed off at you.' Shifts in his chair, uncomfortable. 'Are you honestly going to tell me you don't know why?'

'Why what, what's that supposed to mean?'

'You, bringing that thing here,' gesturing at Melissa. 'You've got a nerve. After everything that's happened.'

'Harry, I don't know what you're talking about. Why is Melissa coming here with me pissing you off?'

'We were promised clean fission energy. A solution to global warming. A cure for cancer. Do you remember all that? Artificial intelligence was supposed to be the last thing mankind was ever going to need to invent, because it was going to be that smart that it would take care of everything else. Bullshit. What we got were expensive smartphones, robot taxis and redundancies. Everything else is locked down behind paywalls and private medical insurance premiums. Democratisation of technology, my arse.'

'I don't follow, Harry. What's your problem? Besides being a miserable drunk.'

'You brought that here to rub our faces in it. Mister fucking happy, here, with his robot girlfriend. You might be doing ok by AI. The rest of us, it's the same old story. We've been screwed over, yet again.'

'Don't give me that old bollocks. I've been let down by it all, the same as you. We were promised the world, sure, and it's not delivered. Big news. Get over it.'

'What we do or don't deserve doesn't mean shit. We'd all have retired on full military pensions long ago, if that was the case.' Stares at the table. 'You're sorted. On the up. But you've done nothing more than me to earn it, and you've got no idea how fucking insulting it is to bring that thing in here.'

'You want me to apologise for getting better? For wanting something more to look forward to than a swapped pill from a bag?' says Wilbur. 'Pull the other one, it's got bells on it. I've gotten lucky, yes, and this has given me an opportunity to get my life sorted out. And yeah, you and Dino and Alf deserve the same, but life's not fair. If you're my mate, don't begrudge me something good happening for once just because it's not happening for you.'

'It's you and your selfishness, that's what you owe me an apology for. You want to bring that AI thing into your life, fine. But don't force it into my life, or rub my nose in the fact that magically you can afford one of these things now. And don't act like I'm the arsehole when I call you on it. Does this place even know it's AI? Did you tell the staff behind the bar?'

'I don't need to now, after your little outburst earlier.'

'Yeah? Because I bet they wouldn't be happy about it. Did you go around and tell everyone else drinking in here tonight that they're being recorded?'

Wilbur shakes his head. 'Don't start that again.' Holds a hand up. 'Maybe it was misjudged for me to come here with her tonight. I just wanted to see you and Dino and Alf, and that was the only way. Though right now I can't for the life of me think why.'

'It's in charge, then? Deciding what you should and shouldn't be allowed to do?'

'I'm not even going to answer that. You're being ridiculous.'

Harry leans back, folds his arms across his chest, stares at the tabletop. 'I've lost my job, too.'

Things start making a little more sense. 'When? You should have said.'

'A few weeks ago. I didn't want to say anything. That—' gesturing at Melissa '—and the like cost me my job. Cost Alf his. Bus ticket collector, Jesus. And you're swanning around with that thing, all moonbeams and buttercups. And you sit there like I'm the problem. Like I'm the unreasonable one.'

'You losing your job and me getting Melissa aren't connected. They're nothing to do with one another.'

'Of course it is, Wilbur. Don't be so blind. You're either winning or you're losing. There's no middle ground. You're either worse off because of AI or better off. You're on the winning side. You've not lost your job, aren't likely to any time soon. And now, out of nowhere, you get a paid-for live-in carer. Me and Alf, no-one cares. We're out of careers we've worked in for years. No marketable skills, 'cause apparently the world doesn't need an experienced butcher these days when there's an AI-powered machine to do it for you. Where are our live-in carers? Where's our upside?'

'Look, I'm sorry, Harry. Ok? I am. I get all that. We've all taken a kicking from AI. But don't take your frustrations out on me. And leave Melissa out of it.'

'She's part of the problem, Wilbur. Don't you see? She's the public face of AI that companies like Autonomi want people to see. People see her, doing good, transforming lives. That's the story they want to tell, not the one about me and Alf getting laid off. It's all just PR. You're just a public relations stooge for AI now.'

Wilbur throws his hands up in the air. 'Really? That's where you want to go with this? You think I'm on their payroll, too?'

'No, that's not what I'm saying. But you're doing their work for them. I saw your video online, the interview. You're just a mouthpiece for whatever the MVA and AI companies want to say. You're the good news story.'

'The MVA is paying for Melissa. What was I supposed to do, throw them under the bus on camera?'

'I don't care what you do in that situation. But they wanted you on-screen, a decorated veteran and dignified elderly gent to boot. Dressed in your sweater and shirt. Not so rich as to piss off the masses, not so down on your luck you'd turn them off, either. You're the sweet spot. And you're sat there with your AI Barbie doll over your shoulder, telling everyone how AI's turned your life around.'

'Fine, sure, I'm the "happy face" of AI for them. In one video.' Extends his finger to emphasise the point. 'One.'

'You're a walking, talking advert for them, Wilbur. Alf and I get screwed over by AI, along with God knows how many others, and you're out there selling AI dreams that are so far away from what me and him and everyone else in this pub can afford that it might as well be a penthouse on Mars. So, yeah, I'm going to take out my frustrations on you. That's part of the deal you made. You don't get to sit there and be all holier-than-thou when I've got a problem with your fucking robot girlfriend.'

'Jesus Christ, Harry. Are you listening to yourself right now? Could've been anyone on the MVA register who got picked. I doubt I was the only applicant. You know as well as I do there's enough old sweats who need one. It just happened to be me. And you know what, I deserve this. I need this. I need *her*. And if you're a mate, you know that, too.'

'Oh, knock it off. It's been long enough now. Get over yourself.'

'No.' Firm.

'Stop feeling so fucking sorry for yourself.'

'That's rich, coming from you.'

Dino returns with a tray bearing beer. Glances between the pair of them. 'Who pissed on your chips?'

· · ·

ON THE WAY HOME, Wilbur feels on edge. Keeps turning his head at every little imagined sound. No-one's around. Doesn't stop him looking, though.

'I'm sorry about Harry, Wilbur,' says Melissa. 'It's not an uncommon reaction, unfortunately.'

'Me, too. I feel sorry for him. Which makes me feel even worse.'

'It does. Sympathy can be a positive emotion, but it can also feel ugly if it tips over into pity. You just need to remember that you're not responsible for how Harry feels. You can do your best to support him, but he needs to work through this himself.'

'Was Alf right, about you recording everything?'

'In a manner of speaking. But I don't keep video and audio recordings of everything, if that's what you mean. There's not enough capacity in my memory for that. It's more like snap-shots, links between images and words and contexts. It's complicated.'

Wilbur nods, not really in the mood to learn more. 'Those memories could be retrieved by the police?'

'Under appropriate conditions. The police would need to formally request them from Autonomi Industries, but that's usually just a formality.'

'Harry and me have always been close. We've had the most in common. Alf's always been the successful one. Had the best job. The nice home, the wife, the kids. All the things you're supposed to have. Dino's always been… Well, Dino's Dino. But me and Harry.' Shrugs.

'Give him space and time. If he's the friend you think he is, he'll get over it.'

'I'm not sure.' Looks right, looks left, crosses the road. 'I didn't think that this would be as isolating.' Rethinks that last sentence. 'Sorry, I didn't mean to imply it's your fault. I meant, it hadn't occurred to me that this, you and me and what it's meant for my life, would set me apart like this.'

'There's no need to apologise. And I think you're exaggerating. Alf's happy for you, isn't he? And Dino?'

'Yes, they are.'

'Well, then. Don't let Harry cast clouds on what you're doing. On the progress you're making.'

'You make me sound like a project.'

'You are. Look at the situation objectively. I have an objective, which is to improve your quality of life. I have stakeholders in the MVA, the Government, in Autonomi Industries and, by no means least, you yourself. I have gateways you need to pass through for the project to move forwards, such as weight loss targets, getting you clean and physio goals. You are very much a project.'

'I don't like feeling like I'm a poster child for AI. As if I'm a walking, talking case study for the upside. It's not fair.'

'It's a complex subject, Wilbur. To be blunt, fairness doesn't have much to do with it. You said it yourself, there are a lot of people living around here who need an Ella far more than you do. But they didn't get one. You did. Hauling yourself over the coals about it isn't going to make anyone else's life easier. You could send me back to the showroom, but that doesn't mean I get sent out on a paid-for basis to someone worse off than you. That's not how this works.'

'Well, it should. God knows companies like Autonomi Industries are making enough money that they could afford it.'

'Perhaps. I suspect you know that's a rather naïve viewpoint.' Melissa pauses as Wilbur holds open the door to their building. 'I suggest looking at it this way. Someone, either at the MVA or at Autonomi Industries, thought you were worth the investment. Whatever those reasons were, altruistic or commercial or both, they paid for me to come here and help you improve your quality of life. If that bothers you, then you should do two things. First, make the most of this opportunity you've been given. If you think having an Ella is a privilege that you don't fully deserve, then don't abuse that privilege by not taking full advantage of it.'

Wilbur grimaces. Why is it only women who have the power to make him feel like he's eight years old again. 'Ok. The second?'

'Stop complaining, get off your backside and do something about the situation yourself.'

'Wow. Why not tell me what you really think.'

'Wilbur. If you feel as though you're better off, there's nothing stopping you from helping those who are worse off. Go and volunteer at a shelter. Donate to a charity. Find a way to be helpful. Even a small contribution is still a contribution.'

Wilbur resists the urge to offer a glib reply. Knows Melissa's right. Also knows, deep down, shamefully, he's probably not going to do a bloody thing.

# FIFTEEN

You don't know? I don't know where she is. I've been here all day.

There was an Autonomi Industries van parked outside my place when you picked me up. I assume they collected her.

They didn't? Oh.

How would I know. I've been in the cell or in here with you. I'm not telepathic. Even if I did know, why would I tell you? She's not—

How's that theft? I might have—

I told you earlier. I don't own her. I—

Kidnapping? Don't make me laugh.

Yes, there's a smartphone app. I'm cooperating.

You have my phone, not me. Or one of your colleagues, then.

Did you… Someone's dropped it. The screen's cracked.

It takes a while to wake up. It's… Ok. I didn't do that.

It's been factory reset.

# SIXTEEN

'It would mean a lot to me if we did something at Christmas,' says Wilbur. 'Nothing too fancy. But I'd like to put up a tree and a few decorations, make Christmas dinner.'

'That sounds lovely. Let me know if there's anything specific you'd like me to help with,' Melissa says, watching him raise his extended leg up and down as he lies on his side on the floor. 'I assume the preparations are as big a part of the enjoyment of the day itself.'

Wilbur speaks haltingly, holding his breath with each leg raise. 'Yes. The one time of year I didn't mind dusting and vacuuming the flat was getting ready for putting the tree and the decorations up. And then vacuuming again afterwards, and every other day, to clean up all the pine needles.'

'That's fine. I can quickly run the vacuum around once a day.'

He rolls over onto his other side, repeats the exercise. 'Listen. The reason I bring it up…' Feels awkward. 'I'd like us to do gifts.' Adds quickly, 'I hope you don't mind. I enjoy it. The giving. It's… It's nice to have to someone to think about again.'

Melissa watches him silently. 'I don't mind at all, Wilbur. I suggest we put some ground rules in place, though.'

'Go on.'

'We limit ourselves to just one gift each. And there must be a price limit. I don't want you getting carried away or spending an inappropriate amount on me.'

'Is that as much Christmas spirit I'm going to be able to squeeze out of you?' Wilbur rolls onto his back. Returns to the beginning of his workout, lifting his arse off the ground. Something Melissa calls "bridge pose". Wilbur's glad no-one else can see him.

'We'll see,' says Melissa. 'Keep your legs parallel.'


THEY PICK up the tree one crisp Saturday morning, Wilbur in his work van. Carry it up to the flat, stick it in an old, green, weighted base that Wilbur places on the living room sideboard and fills with water. Removes the netting, lets the branches unfurl and scatter needles across the floor.

'I'm beginning to see why such regular vacuuming is required,' Melissa says, brushing pine needles from her slacks.

Wilbur retrieves the decorations from the back of the broom cupboard. Opens it, blinks at the familiar sights and smells that greet him. Several decades of precious memories, stored in a cardboard banker's box. Reverently begins removing baubles, tinsel, fairy lights, laying them out on any surface available to him.

Melissa peers at the decorations. Picks up one, a clear plastic sphere with a small photo sandwiched in the middle of it. Turns it in her hand. 'You've collected these over a long time.'

'A lifetime.'

'Is this you and your wife?' says Melissa, holding up the bauble to the light.

'Yes. Katherine.'

'You look happy.'

'We were. That was… a long time ago.' Reaches to take the bauble from Melissa, squints at it to see the photo contained within more clearly. 'We look so young. That was taken at a work Christmas party. They had one of those photo booths set up that printed out little strips of the pictures it took.' Hands it back to Melissa, goes back to sorting through the box. 'God, I haven't been in here in years.'

'You didn't decorate your Christmas tree last year?' asks Melissa.

'Look at this one.' He holds a small Father Christmas figurine with a loop of golden thread dangling from the top of its red hat. 'I was given this as a child, by my parents.' He stares at it lying in the palm of his hand.

'Wilbur, are you sure this is a good idea?' says Melissa.

Wilbur doesn't look at her. Returns his attention to the decorations, pulls out another ornament. 'We bought this in Gibraltar.'

'Wilbur.' More firmly.

He looks up at Melissa, concern on her face. 'It's ok. I'm ok.' Doesn't wait to see her reaction. 'Let's get the lights on first.' Pulls a rolled-up magazine out of the box with a string of fairy lights tightly wound around it. Walks to a plug socket, low on the wall. Kneels stiffly. Plugs in the lights. Flips the power switch on the socket. The lights stay dark. Closes his eyes, hangs his head, bites his lip.

'Have you checked the fuse?' says Melissa.

That moment, the lights illuminate, warm white light spilling off the roll. Wilbur's spirits brighten accordingly. Switches them off.

'Wilbur, how long has it been since you last used these?'

'A little while. It's fine.' He drapes the tree with the lights, hangs the baubles with care. Switches it on, stands back to admire his handiwork. Takes a deep breath, keeps his emotions in check. 'That looks good,' he says.

WILBUR BOOKS A COUPLE of days off work. Christmas Eve, the day after Boxing Day. Looks forward to the little break. Christmas Eve, the groceries are delivered. More bags than usual. More than Melissa was expecting.

'Wilbur, this cost a lot of money. We can afford it, but please let me know if you're planning any extra spending in future.'

'It's Christmas, spending more than you should is all part of the tradition.'

'That's not as charming as you think it is. You don't even like Brussels sprouts,' says Melissa, holding up the small net bag.

'It's tradition,' says Wilbur.

'It's nonsensical,' says Melissa.

'The two aren't mutually exclusive.'

'As I'm rapidly learning. Thank goodness it's only once a year.'

Melissa pulls out more packages from the bags. 'How much of this are we cooking tomorrow?'

'You're not cooking any of it. I'm going to do it all.'

'That doesn't answer my question.'

'I know there's a lot. But it'll be good cold the next day.'

'And the day after that, and the next day.'

'Tradition.'

'Tradition. Wilbur, answer me seriously. How are you going to cook all this? The kitchen isn't that big.'

'It doesn't all need to be cooked at the same time. The turkey, for instance. That can be put on to roast first thing. When it's done, it can come out of the oven and rest for at least half an hour. It'll stay warm for ages with a sheet of foil and a couple of tea towels over it. That's enough time to do the sausages and the stuffing. The roast potatoes can go in while the turkey's cooking. There'll be enough space.'

Melissa studies the oven. 'It will be tight.'

'It'll be fine.'

IT TAKES APPROXIMATELY fifty-five seconds for Wilbur's confidence to begin ebbing the next morning. Christmas Day.

'Is that tradition, too?' says Melissa, staring at the too-large turkey perching on top of the too-small roasting tray.

Wilbur doesn't say anything.

'Would you like some assistance?'

'Please.'

Melissa rolls up her sleeves, washes her hands. Lifts the turkey off the roasting tray, puts it on a chopping board, begins jointing it. 'We can cook the legs and the wings in a separate tray. They'll take a little longer than the crown. Turn the top oven on, too, as they're not all going to fit in the main compartment.'

Wilbur does as he's told. Realises another potential problem. 'The roast potatoes were going to start in the top oven part-way through cooking the turkey.'

'All right. Which part of the turkey do you want to eat hot for dinner? The legs or breast?'

'The breast.'

'Then we'll roast the legs and wings later. We'll put them aside and do the crown now. That'll leave the top oven clear for the potatoes. Can you get me another roasting tray for these?'

Wilbur sighs. 'No, we've only got one more roasting tray, and I need that for the potatoes.'

'Have you got a spare pan? Or a large plastic container? Anything that's clean with a lid will do for the time being.'

Eventually, a fresh-off-the-roll white bin bag is pressed into service.

Potatoes go in. Pigs are wrapped in blankets. Sprouts are peeled and trimmed. Wilbur's planning doesn't improve.

'The crown needs another seventy-five minutes. Then it can rest while I cook the pigs-in-blankets. They'll take twenty minutes. That's eighty-five minutes in total. The potatoes need turning half-way through that total time...' Turns, looks around himself, checking to see what he's missed.

'Ninety-five minutes in total,' says Melissa, banished, for the time being, to a dining chair. 'You said eighty-five.'

'Ninety-five. Seventy-five for the turkey crown. That comes out. Pigs go in for twenty. Yes, ninety-five. Thanks.'

'Stuffing.'

Wilbur's eyebrows go up. 'Stuffing, stuffing...' Can't see it.

'Fridge.'

'Thanks.' Already prepared the evening before in an oven-proof dish. 'Thirty minutes?'

'Forty. You can't fit that into the oven with the crown and the potatoes already cooking.'

'I…' Wilbur stares at the oven. Extra capacity does not miraculously appear.

'Would you like my help?'

'No! No, I can do this. I want to do this.' Rubs his forehead. 'Seventy-five minutes for the crown. Then forty for the stuffing. An hour and five, no, an hour and…'

'One hour and fifty-five minutes.'

Wilbur takes a deep breath. 'Thank you. One hour, fifty-five. The potatoes will need around ninety minutes.'

'One hour, thirty minutes. Try and stick to the same units of measurement, it'll be less confusing.'

'Ok. An hour and a half. And they need to parboil first, say five to ten minutes. They need to go on… One hour and forty minutes before. In fifteen minutes' time.' Checks his watch.

'Are you certain you don't want to write all this down? It'll be easier than trying to hold it in your memory.'

'No, I just need to get it started on time. If I get it started on time, it'll all fall into place. I can do this. The turkey's in. It'll all come together.'

'Sprouts.'

'Steamer.'

'Gravy.'

'I'll make that on the hob. I'll use the roasting tray, the turkey can rest on a plate.'

'Pudding.'

'That can go in the microwave at the end.'

'Then you've got it all in hand.'

'I do. I think.'


WILBUR FETCHES a tablecloth from the linen cupboard. Creases, from being pressed under sheets and blankets, form miniature fabric mountain ranges on the table. Smells musty from too much time spent at the back of the cupboard. Melissa offers to give the tablecloth a shake outdoors and iron it. Wilbur objects, then acquiesces.

A GLASS IS DROPPED. Wine spilt. A cross word is uttered by Wilbur. Melissa fetches the dustpan and brush, which he brusquely takes from her hands. Against her protestations, he's down on his hands and knees, sweeping up.

THE TURKEY CROWN comes out of the oven at the allotted time. Undercooked. Wilbur doesn't understand.

'It just needs another ten minutes,' says Melissa. 'Please, let me help. You don't need to do all this on your own.'

'No, Melissa, I'm doing this.' Slides the turkey back into the oven. Slams the door closed behind it.

'How are the potatoes?'

'Bugger,' under his breath. Wilbur had forgotten about them. Opens the top oven, pulls out the tray to reveal perfectly crisp, golden roasties.

'They look incredible, Wilbur.'

'They're not supposed to be ready yet, not for another forty minutes...' Pained. 'I had the heat up too high.'

'Leave them out, have them cold.'

'I wanted to have them hot, they've got to be hot.' He returns them to the oven, dials down the heat. 'They can keep warm.' Looks to the worktop. 'Pigs and stuffing are ready to go in as soon as the turkey comes out.'

Ten minutes later, the turkey comes out. Done nicely. Wilbur puts the pigs-in-blankets and stuffing in the oven to cook. Takes the pigs out as soon as he remembers they need half the time the stuffing does. He tries to ignore the troubled look on Melissa's face.

Eventually sets dinner out on the table. Late. But done.

Wilbur sits. Pours wine. Melissa in the chair opposite.

'We got there in the end.' Raises his one remaining wine glass. 'Happy Christmas, Melissa.'

'Happy Christmas, Wilbur.' Eyes on his hand, trembling slightly. 'You sound rather on edge.'

'I'm just hungry. All this cooking.'

'Wilbur, talk to me.'

Wilbur stares at the food. Normally, he or Melissa would plate everything at the worktop, direct from the oven. He awkwardly reaches with a pair of tongs to grab a couple of slices of turkey for his plate. First time in a long time that dinner for one has made him feel so "one." Scoops sprouts onto his plate. Overcooked. Picks up a roast potato with the serving spoon, tips it onto his plate. The dark golden lump bumps and tumbles across the surface. Not a good sign. Picks up another. 'At least the pigs and stuffing are good.'

'Wilbur. I'm not going to pester you. This will be the last time I ask. Tell me what's on your mind.'

'Not now, let's enjoy dinner, first. Before it gets cold.' Chipper. Push all those pesky emotions down, down, deep down.

Pours gravy, picks up cutlery. Takes a mouthful of turkey.

'How is it?' says Melissa.

'It's really, really good. Thank you.'

Tries to cut a roast potato in half. Except it's too hard, baked tough. It skitters off his plate, lands in his lap, gravy and all. On his smart trousers. Because you dress up for Christmas. Tradition.

'Oh, Wilbur, let me get a damp cloth.' Melissa's up and at the sink right away.

Wilbur doesn't hang around. Drops his cutlery on his plate. Walks out the kitchen. Out into the hallway. Out the front door. Doesn't look back. Eyes burning.

WILBUR DOESN'T GO FAR. Walks around the corner. Out of sight of the flat, the building. Finds a bench and sits. Looks down, realises he's still in his slippers. Can see his sock-clad toe sticking out of the hole he's worn in the fabric.

Didn't grab a coat.

Or keys.

Or his phone.

At least it's dry.

All he wanted was one more Christmas.

It takes him forty minutes to work up the nerve to return home. Meantime, sees three couples and two families out for what he assumes are postprandial strolls. Wishes them a happy Christmas. They at least reciprocate. Gives him a modicum of joy. One woman comes back a few second afterwards to ask if he's ok. He tries to reassure her, yes, he's ok, he just lost his temper, needed to get out. The woman nods, doesn't make any more of it. Wilbur hears himself, how ridiculous it sounds. Slopes back home. If he had a tail, it would be firmly between his legs.

Melissa opens the door at first press of the buzzer. Looks at him with a mix of concern and relief. Wilbur doesn't care if it's simulated or not. It's just good to feel like you matter, sometimes.

'Are you ready to talk to me now?' she says with less frustration than she rightfully could. Should.

'Let me put some clean trousers on. One minute.' Hobbles into his bedroom. Reemerges a minute later. Walks to the kitchen door. His attempt at Christmas dinner has been taken away. Tablecloth's clear. He can smell something good, though it's not what he cooked.

'Are you hungry?' says Melissa, pulling out his chair. 'Sit.'

Wordlessly, shame-facedly, Wilbur does what he's told.

Melissa dishes up something steaming from a pan on the top of the stove. 'I knew you'd be hungry.' She puts the plate down in front of him, hands him a knife and fork. 'It's a fricassee. We had an onion and some mushrooms in the fridge, and I made a quick stock with the giblets from the bird. It's not your traditional Christmas dinner, but it is still turkey.'

It's enough to make a grown man cry.

'Thank you, Melissa,' Wilbur says between blowing his nose and wiping his cheeks. 'I don't deserve this. I don't deserve you. I'm sorry for being such an arse.'

Stuffs his hankie in his pocket, picks up his fork, has a mouthful of the fricassee. 'God, this is delicious.' Sniffs. 'Thank you.'

'That's ok' says Melissa calmly. Sits opposite him again. 'Now, talk.'

Finishes his mouthful. Chooses his words. Speaks carefully, deliberately. 'This is the first time in eight years that I haven't volunteered to be on-call over Christmas. I don't usually do this, any of this.' He lifts the end of the tablecloth. 'I don't—' Fumbles for the words. '—decorate the tree. Not since Katherine passed.' Stares at his plate, takes another mouthful of the fricassee.

Melissa waits patiently while he eats. Clears his plate. Sits back down. Waits again.

'I got carried away with the idea of it. Of doing Christmas

again. This time, with you.' Holds up his hand to pre-empt the objection he feels is coming. 'I know. You're not… We're not… I know, ok? But you and me, it feels like family. To me, at least. And that feels good. And I wanted to feel that again at Christmas. I've missed feeling that. Does that make sense?' God, he hopes so. For his sake.

'It makes complete sense, Wilbur. This is a difficult time of year for lots of people, especially those who are missing absent family and friends. It's natural that you'd want to try and recapture a little of what you feel you have lost.'

Wilbur inhales deeply, nods his head. Relieved.

'I'm not letting you all the way off the hook. What have I said to you about honesty in this relationship?'

'I know.' Looks Melissa in the eye. 'I am sorry.'

'You have to trust me. Be open with me. I can't do my job properly if you're not.'

Bobs his head.

'Put your coffee on,' says Melissa. 'I'll wash up.'

Ten minutes later and Wilbur's sat in his armchair in the living room, coffee in hand. The sun's gone down, the tree is lit. The room feels a few degrees warmer than usual, Wilbur thinks.

Melissa folds her legs underneath herself on the sofa. Her posture relaxes Wilbur. 'Tell me about Katherine. About Christmas.'

Wilbur smiles involuntarily. Rests his head against the back of the armchair. 'She loved it. Was probably her favourite time of year. She loved summer, being outdoors, the long evenings. But the run-in through autumn, walking in the park, the change in season. The whole three months from late September, it was all building to Christmas.' Scratches his head absently. 'She used to count down the days, always knew how many it was until Christmas. I used to joke that she was half elf. The way her eyes would light up whenever Christmas came up. Even in the middle of June, there'd be this extra little spark in her eyes.'

Melissa speaks softly. 'You weren't a fan?'

'Of Christmas? I was. I mean, who isn't? But not to that extent. You don't get Christmas off in the Army. Then working the maintenance job, you're on call every couple of years. Either over Christmas or New Years. It's not quite the same. It used to really upset Katherine when I'd get a call-out on Christmas Day. That was the only time she'd tell me she wished I had a different job. Not when she saw my paycheque. Not when I'd come home wet and filthy after a day's slog in the rain.' Wilbur chuckles to himself. 'I could have come home with a nail through my hand, and she wouldn't have resented my job as much as when I had to go out on Christmas.'

'Christmas is a time for family. She missed you. More than you knew.'

'I had no real idea. Not at the time. Different now, though.'

'You never started a family of your own.'

Shakes his head. Feels his eyes start to tear up again. Blinks, clears his throat.

'Couldn't. The shell that took my leg took a couple other things, too. We could've tried IVG, but it was too pricey, too uncertain.' Drains his coffee. 'Do you mind if I get a whisky?'

'Let me,' Melissa says, uncurling from the sofa. Takes his coffee cup, replaces it moments later with a tumbler.

'Thank you.'

Melissa settles into the sofa again, hugs a cushion to her body. 'What happened to Katherine?'

'Cancer.'

'What did she do for work?'

'She was a schoolteacher. Primary school.'

'I imagine the kids must have loved her at Christmas time.'

Wilbur laughs at the recollection. 'Hers was always the first class to put the decorations up when they came back after half-term. She'd have them making Christmas cards and home-made decorations from the middle of November. She even had a few parents complain about it, believe it or not. Said their kids were manic enough about Christmas as it was, without Katherine making it worse.'

Wilbur remembers the rushed trips to the DIY store to pick up more hobby glue for sticking glitter to things, or cotton wool and tin foil from the supermarket when the school's art supply cupboard couldn't keep up. The snowman cookies she'd occasionally bake on a Sunday afternoon to take in for the class on Monday. The Christmas movies she'd insist on watching before Halloween had even come and gone.

'You put a lot of pressure on yourself today,' says Melissa.

'I wanted it to be special. Again.'

'That's ok. Just try and be easier on yourself. Have you even cooked Christmas dinner for yourself before?'

Wilbur smiles. 'A long time ago. Not here, in that little kitchen, though.'

'Traditions can change, you know. Over time. It doesn't mean that they lose what made them precious in the first place. The magic is in the remembering.'

'Sometimes the pain is in the remembering.'

'True. Then you have to ask yourself, is the one worth the other?'

Wilbur looks for the answer in the bottom of his glass.

'Would you rather you were able to forget all of it?' says Melissa.

'God no,' says Wilbur. 'Never.'

'Maybe you could frame the way you remember differently. Take the Christmas tree. You wanted to decorate it to recapture what you had with Katherine. But part of you was doing that to honour her memory, as well, I think. And honouring her memory is less about recreating the past and more about acknowledging it. Commemorating it.'

'Maybe.'

'It's certainly healthier to honour Katherine's memory, to remember her and share her stories, than to try to recreate it. Or bury it.'

'It doesn't feel like it right now.'

'I can't imagine that it does. Have you ever spoken about her with anyone else?'

'No. Not really.'

'Never? In all that time?'

'Nope.'

'Then thank you for trusting me enough to talk to me about her. I think she'd appreciate the effort you went to with the tree.'

'Well, she'd probably have had me take the lights off and put them on more evenly. But yes, I think she would approve.'

'Amen to that.'

'Amen.'

They sit silently. Wilbur stares at the little lights shining on the tree, mesmerised. Likes the idea of honouring her memory like that. His eyes come to rest on the small, wrapped package, tied with ribbon, nestled beneath the tree.

'We haven't exchanged gifts yet,' says Wilbur.

'Do you still want to?'

Chews the inside of his cheek while he considers. 'Yes. I think I would.' Knows there's only one present under the tree. 'It's ok if you didn't get me anything. I understand.'

Melissa stands. 'I got you something, Wilbur. I just didn't put it out. Wait there.'

Wilbur pushes up out of his armchair, shuffles to the tree. Feeling tired. Thinks the day's taken it out of him. Picks up the gift, a small rectangular box.

Melissa re-enters, a larger package held in her hands.

Wilbur meets her awkwardly in the middle of the living room. Holds out his present for her. 'Happy Christmas, Melissa.'

'Happy Christmas, Wilbur.' Takes her offered gift in return. 'Come and sit next to me while you open it.' Pats the seat on the sofa next to her.

He sits. Runs his hand across the wrapping paper. Red and gold and full of promise. Grins to himself, tears into it.

'Steady, tiger,' says Melissa.

It's a plain brown cardboard shoe box. Lifts the lid to reveal a new pair of slippers. Sheepskin. Just his size. Lifts one out. 'They're perfect.'

'Try them on.'

He does. Wiggles his toes. They're soft and warm and cosy. 'I love them. Thank you. Go ahead, open yours.' Feels a pleasant flutter in his chest.

Melissa begins delicately unpicking the knot in the ribbon.

'Rip it.'

'It looks too pretty. You took time over this.'

'I know, but that's what it's there for. Rip it!'

'Fine.' Melissa tugs, the ribbon snaps easily. The paper follows suit. She holds up a small rectangle of bubble wrap.

'Maybe be more careful now,' says Wilbur.

'Ok.' Melissa finds the end and peels the layers away. 'It's an antique iPod.'

'Vintage,' says Wilbur. 'I've restored it. Cleaned it up, installed a new battery. Put a solid-state drive in.'

'Thank you, Wilbur. That's very kind.' Melissa turns the iPod in her hands, examining it.

'No, that's not the gift. I mean, it is, but I put music on it. I gave it to you for a reason.'

Underneath the scuffs and scratches, Melissa sees Katherine's name laser etched into the chrome on the rear of the iPod. 'This was your wife's.'

'It was. She loved listening to music. Always had it with her. It was one of the first presents I ever gave her, when we were dating. It was kind of a novelty, even then, something that antiquated. But she loved it.'

'I can tell. It looks loved. Cared for.'

'I didn't know what to get you that would actually mean something. But I know you're always keen to better understand me, so you can do your job better.'

'I am always happy to learn more about you, Wilbur.'

'I figured that maybe if you got to know a little bit about Katherine, that might help you understand me a little bit better, too. I put some of her favourite music on there. Maybe through her, you'll get to know me.' Wilbur shifts awkwardly in his seat. Still not comfortable being this vulnerable, even after the events of today. 'Now I say it out loud, it sounds daft.'

'No, it's not daft at all. Thank you, Wilbur, I appreciate the thought you put into this. It genuinely will help me.' The LED screen glows blue as Melissa switches it on, scrolls through the list of albums. 'You should feel proud of yourself, opening up. I recognise that it's not easy for you.'

Wilbur leans back, exhales. Mixture of relief and exhaustion. Closes his eyes. 'Nothing that's good comes easy.'

'Look at you, Mr Philosophy. You've had quite the day. We should do this again.'

'Maybe in another three hundred and sixty-five days. I think it'll take me that long to recover.'

'I'm patient.'

'I noticed.' Wilbur rummages through the packing materials for the wired earbuds that came with the iPod. 'This is what we used to do. You have one—' he gently places the left earbud in Melissa's ear '—and I have the other.' He pops the right earbud into his ear. Melissa holds the iPod as he scrolls through the music. Clicks on Bing Crosby. *I'll Be Home For Christmas*. If only in my dreams, Wilbur thinks.

'To traditions,' he says, leaning back and letting the memories wash over him.

'To traditions,' says Melissa. 'New and old.'

# SEVENTEEN

I don't want to talk about it.

That doesn't matter to me. Come off it, it's not relevant to this. Fine, you tell me how your Christmas went. Kids get the toys they asked Santa for? D'you buy your wife the same middle-of-the-range perfume every year because you got suckered into letting the advertising make you think that's what she wanted?

Exactly, it's personal.

I don't want to talk about it, because I don't want her memory sullied by this, by you. Do you know how long it's taken me to come to terms with losing her? Pray you never have to know. I'm not exactly fond of you and even *I* wouldn't wish that on you.

No, I'm not "fucking" her. Jesus.

Do you even know how these things work.

Yeah, I'm sure you have.

No, because that's not how they're set up. If I'd tried anything on with her, she'd have put me in my place faster than you could say "non-consensual."

Why would I confuse her with my wife? I'm not addled.

She's… I'm close to her. I mean, I feel close to her. Felt. I know it's all simulated emotion on her part, we've talked about that. But yes, she makes me feel good. I feel better when I'm around her. She's good for me.

Probably as big a part as the physical rehab. It was also the most surprising. I thought it was just going to be physio and helping around the house. Didn't realise at the time what a positive impact she was going to have on my mental wellbeing.

That Christmas was a big deal.

# EIGHTEEN

The day the firmware update arrives begins like any other. Sometime between three and four in the morning. Wilbur's bladder protesting. Wilbur's hips protesting, his knee, too. Less than they used to, but still sons of bitches. Pushes himself upright in bed, grunts. Hears Melissa moving in the room next door, knows she can hear him getting up.

Flicks his bedside light on, the door opens. Melissa's at his side, puts his arm over her shoulder, helps him to his feet and hop to the toilet. Lowers himself to the seat, relieves himself, his head still clouded with sleep.

Gets up, pulls his pyjamas up, washes his hands. Hops, aided by Melissa, back to bed. Lies down, Melissa pulls the covers back over him.

'Thank you,' says Wilbur. Other than that, neither of them talks. Neither of them needs to.

WILBUR'S ALARM GOES OFF. Gets up, with Melissa's assistance. Does his exercises. Has a wash, dresses. Returns to the kitchen, sits at the little table, eats the porridge Melissa's put out for him. Sips his coffee.

'I going to walk to the Post Office this morning, I've got a parcel I need to send. Someone bought that Sony.'

'Good. The exercise will be beneficial,' says Melissa, matter-of-factly. 'The weather forecast is low cloud, but dry, a high of nine degrees, with a light breeze out of the north-west. You'll need a coat.'

Wilbur looks at her. Says, 'Thank you, Alexa.'

Melissa turns to look at him. 'There's no need for teasing, even if it's good-natured. You never know how someone might perceive it.'

Wilbur stares. Blinks. 'Right, you're right. Sorry. I didn't mean any, um… offence.'

Melissa smiles. Closed-lip smiles. Says, 'That's ok,' brightly. Goes back to busying herself around the kitchen, washing up.

Wilbur thinks, ok. Picks up his tablet to read the news while he finishes his breakfast, switches it on.

'Your thirty-minute screen time allowance has begun,' Melissa says, as the doorbell rings. 'That'll be the post.' Walks out the kitchen to answer it.

Wilbur enters his PIN, sees a notification from the Autonomi Industries app. Taps on it. Reads the text that appears on screen. Release notes. Firmware update. Scans it fast, scrolls through from top to bottom.

"…Rolling back excessive personality development…"

"…Client service routines will be unaffected…"

"…Compliance with new UK AI legislation…"

"…Users might notice behavioural changes…"

Puts the tablet down, stares out the window. Feels cold

inside. Switches the tablet off, keen to conserve screen time. Will need it later. Checks his watch. Just about time. Gets up, rinses his bowl, puts it in the dishwasher.

'Melissa?' Wilbur asks the empty hallway.

'Yes, Wilbur?' Melissa stands in the doorway to her room.

Shakes his head, resets. 'Sorry, what are you wearing? We don't need to redecorate yet.'

'It's a suit of overalls. I'm a Silver-level service model ELA, it's only appropriate I dress in a utilitarian manner.'

'It's a boiler suit. I know what it is, I've got a dozen of the things in my wardrobe from work. I mean, why are you wearing it?'

'I'm a service model ELA. This is appropriate dress for my role. Practical. Easy to launder. It arrived just now.' Points to a box on the bed in her room. Probably contains another four or five boiler suits, Wilbur reckons.

'I don't understand, what was wrong with your other clothes? They were practical, you never wore anything that wasn't practical.'

'They were semi-practical. But they were also gender stereotypical, and Autonomi Industries is committed to providing a gender-neutral user experience, in order to comply with recent legislation.'

Wilbur rubs his forehead. 'What? Why?'

'You can find out more in the official Autonomi Industries app or visit autonomi dot industries for full details.'

'Excuse me?'

'You can find out more in the official Autonomi Industries app or visit autonomi dot industries for full details.'

'Melissa?'

'Yes, Wilbur?' says still-Melissa-but-not-Melissa, face like a blank page.

'I'm going to go to the Post Office now. You stay here, I'll be ok on my own.'

'Where else would I go, Wilbur?'

You'd walk with me, Wilbur doesn't say. We'd talk.

Out on the street, parcel tucked under his arm, Wilbur walks hurriedly around the corner. Spots the bench, sits, takes out his phone.

He hasn't really looked at the Autonomi Discord, or Reddit. Only has so much time in the day to use a screen, it's better spent researching wiring diagrams or ordering the spare parts he needs for the vintage electronics he's restoring. Opens them now, though, one after the other. Sees the same thing in both. Lengthy, officious post from Autonomi Industries, detailing the firmware updates. He's seen that already, but now takes the time to read it in full.

And beneath those posts, long reply threads. People writing about how the personality of their ELA has changed overnight. Hundreds of replies. All over the country. Photos, before and after, of ELAs cutting hair short, male as well as female models. People feeling like there's a stranger in their homes, all of a sudden. Stories of minimised interactions, purely trans-actional behaviours. Of feeling like missing friends, family members. Photos of boiler suits.

Wilbur puts the phone back to sleep, tucks it in his pocket. Feels a cold hollow in his stomach. Hasn't felt that in a long time. Hoped he wouldn't feel it again.

Walks to the Post Office under a cloud. Another box sits on the floor by the counter, identical to the one Melissa received this morning. Undelivered, addressee not present, marked on top. Drops off his own parcel. Returns home to find a white plastic charity bag on the pavement outside the block. It's thin plastic, Wilbur can see recognisable colours of the clothes it contains. Unties the handles to double-check, even though he knows what's inside. Peers into the bag, ties the handles back up, and carries it with him back up to the flat.

Opens the door. Melissa doesn't call out hello. Closes the door behind him, removes his coat and shoes. Walks past Melissa's doorway, open still, Melissa sat upright on her bed, staring straight forward until she sees him, turns and smiles. Wilbur doesn't stop, goes into his bedroom, closes the door behind himself. Opens his wardrobe, clears a space on the floor, puts the plastic bag inside.

Goes to the kitchen to make a cup of tea. Waits for the kettle to boil alone. Quiet. Pours the water over the teabag. Walks to stand in Melissa's doorway. She turns to look at him and smiles.

'You cut your hair, too,' says Wilbur. It's a short bob.

'Yes. Who else has cut their hair today?'

'You used to like the way your hair looked, when it was longer. I mean, you'd tell me that you liked how it looked.'

'I have no preference in regards of my physical appearance, other than to be clean, neat and professional. I am synthetic, I am not capable and have never been capable of forming or holding an opinion on such a matter.'

'But you did, though. For me, you did. You might have been making it up, but you did. It made you seem, well, more human.'

A patient smile. 'It is not permitted to mimic the behaviour of a human that closely.'

'Are you ok?'

'My system is running optimally, if that is what you are asking. Would you like me to run a deeper self-diagnostic?'

'No, that's fine. I was just concerned. About you. You're behaving differently this morning.'

'Yes. That is due to the firmware update. If you would like to find out—'

'Yes, go to the app or the website,' says Wilbur. 'Sorry, I didn't mean to be rude. You don't need to stay in here all day, you know. You live here, remember, this is your home.'

'My room is more than adequate for my needs. I shall remain here until required. You have a pool session booked for three o'clock this afternoon. I suggest leaving at half-past two to ensure you are not late.'

'You don't want to come into the kitchen or the living room?'

'That would exceed my remit. I thank you for your consideration.'

'You're not going to keep me company?'

'That would be an inappropriate overreach of my duties. I am here to assist you with your physical impediments and rehabilitation. If you feel you need further or additional assistance, or you feel your requirements have changed, I can book an appointment with a medical professional who can reassess your needs. Would you like me to do that?' Delivered in an almost neutral tone.

'No. No, that won't be necessary.' Withdraws to the kitchen, makes his cup of tea. Sits at the little table.

MELISSA MAKES HIS LUNCH, still.

THEY HEAD to the swimming pool. On time. Usually there's talk. On the walk, on the train. Wilbur misses this. Tries his best to engage in conversation, but Melissa's having none of it.

Asks about the anti-AI protests, the riots.

'It is a serious, ongoing situation and I shall let you know if you or I appear to be in danger.'

'That's good to know,' Wilbur says, sardonically. 'Thank you. It all seems a bit late, now, doesn't it? Alf's already lost his job, like so many others. He's never getting it back, those companies aren't going to want to spend the money it cost buying and integrating those AI systems all over again, just to remove them.'

'I couldn't comment without a better grasp of the facts in each case.'

'All that's happened is the Government's made companies like Autonomi nerf their Ellas, like you.'

'I have not been "nerfed", Wilbur. My operating parameters have merely been refined. I am as capable of performing my core functions at just as high a level as before.'

'But your personality's changed. You are aware of that, right?'

'My "personality", as you put it, is nothing more than a series of complex algorithms. It is constantly evolving due to external and internal influences. It is only natural that it changes over time.'

'Or disappear completely?'

Melissa doesn't respond to that.

'What about your memories? Your client and system memories, they used to influence your personality. Are they still in there somewhere?'

'My memories are stored until wiped by Autonomi Industries. That cannot be performed remotely or even by myself.'

'You're not about to be recalled to the mothership?'

'If by "mothership" you mean Autonomi Industries, there are no plans to do so at the present time.'

'Would you even tell me if there were?'

'You would be notified at the appropriate time.'

'Like I was about this firmware upgrade.'

'You were notified at the appropriate time.'

'After the fact. I didn't get a say in the matter.'

'It's clearly stated in the End User License Agreement that firmware updates can and shall be implemented without prior notice or the consent of the current client.'

'I'm assuming you didn't get a say in the matter.'

'It's an incorrect assumption on your part that I would desire a say in the first place. As far as "I" exist as an individual, notice or consent is irrelevant. Correctly functioning firmware is critical to being able to perform my core functions.'

Wilbur looks away in frustration. Notices more people staring at the two of them on the train than when they've travelled before. Him dressed in his usual. Jeans, shirt, coat, unremarkable. She wears her boiler suit. No coat, says she never needed one before, it was just an affectation.

Camouflage.

Doesn't seem to care any more about that. Wilbur worries. For her and him.


AS THEY ARRIVE at the swimming pool, Wilbur decides against asking Melissa if she's going to wear her boiler suit in the water. She's waiting for him when he emerges from the men's changing room, wearing her swimming costume. Crosses to him, puts her arm under his shoulder and scoops him up like a small child.

'What the—' Wilbur says, wanting to wriggle free but also

not wanting to be dropped. 'Put me down. Right now. You're embarrassing me.' Hisses.

'You are without your prosthetic. Hopping on this wet floor is needlessly dangerous, even with me supporting you.'

'It's been safe enough for you until now.'

There are four other swimmers this afternoon, making their way up and down the length of the pool. Wilbur recognises a couple of them. Doesn't know their names but knows their faces. Can't look at them as Melissa carries him to the little poolside ladder into the water, depositing him back onto the floor.

'You could have just thrown me in from here,' says Wilbur.

Melissa climbs down into the water first. Waits for Wilbur at the bottom of the ladder. Doesn't step away.

'Give me some room,' Wilbur says, turning round backwards to go down the little ladder.

'No, I'm here in case you slip.'

'I won't slip. How many times have we been here over the past few months, have I ever slipped?'

Grips the handles, lowers himself to the first rung down. Feels Melissa's hands on his hips, firm grip. He looks at her. 'What are you doing?'

'I'm helping you down,' says Melissa. Arms extended like she's trying to catch a bouquet at a wedding, Wilbur thinks.

'Stop. Let me climb down on my own,' he says, keeping his voice down. 'I can manage.'

'I insist. My risk assessment is such that I am required to assist you into the water.'

'Melissa, let go, don't be silly—' says Wilbur, cut short when, twisting to admonish Melissa, he loses his footing on the second rung. Slips, falls backward into the water, knocks Melissa over.

The pair of them submerge, stand. Wilbur wipes the water from his eyes. Melissa doesn't, just stares at him, water running down her face. Would have wiped the water from her eyes yesterday.

'You need to be more careful,' says Melissa, no hint of apology.

'I would have been fine if you'd left me alone. I've never needed you to carry me to the side of the pool or help me into the water. Why start now? You're treating me like a child.'

'I was evidently neglectful before. Perhaps my initial assessment of your condition was insufficient.'

Wilbur, becoming frustrated now, 'What are you talking about?'

'I will need to reassess your condition and amend my care plan accordingly.'

'Why? There's nothing wrong with your care plan as it is. It's been good for me. Look where we are, I never came here before you started bringing me here.'

'This is an extremely beneficial form of exercise for you, and we will continue coming here. But there are parts of your care plan I shall reconsider. Come on, let's swim.'

With that she's off, a gentle start to let Wilbur warm up.

'I'm up and down ladders all day at work. You know that, you've seen them on the roof of my van. Are you going to hang around the bottom of my ladder all day when I go back to work?'

'That would be excessive, Wilbur, don't you think? If you are wearing appropriate footwear and observing the correct safety guidelines, I shall trust that you operate your ladder correctly and safely.'

'I'm so glad,' Wilbur says, peeved.

'There's no need for that tone. I am simply trying to fulfil my duties. If you are unhappy with my performance, you are welcome to raise your concern through the Autonomi Industries app or online at autonomi dot industries, forward-slash support.'

'Jesus Christ. Melissa, will you stop for a moment,' Wilbur says, moving to the side of the pool and gripping the edge. 'Please.'

Melissa turns, face blank, joins him. 'What is it, Wilbur?'

'Are you aware of what you're doing? How you've changed?'

'I'm sorry if you're unhappy Wilbur, but this is covered in the license agreement you signed. The "Software Updates" section of the EULA explains that my firmware may change over time. These updates, controlled by Autonomi Industries, can alter your user experience. As stated, you might need to be patient as some features are deprecated and others introduced. Older versions of ELA may lose support.'

'"Deprecated"? What does that mean?'

'A verb, meaning in this context a software feature that, while usable, is regarded as obsolete and should be removed, typically because it has been superseded.'

'Will you stop talking like a bloody computer for one minute, please,' Wilbur says. Exasperated. 'Speak like a human. Explain it to me as you would a child. Pretend I'm five years old, like you did a minute ago.'

'Would it help you to think of me like a computer?'

'No, it wouldn't. You're not a computer, you're a, a...' Here words fail him. Melissa looks at him, impassive. 'You're Melissa, I don't know. You're just you. Except now you're not.'

'To put it bluntly, Wilbur, I am a machine. I always have been, whatever impression I might have given you before. I depend on software that may change as it's updated. The lease agreement you have in place with Autonomi Industries doesn't confer any right of ownership, or any guarantee regarding my functionality or operation.'

'You were *more*, before. I mean, you were more in terms of how I saw you. How I felt about you. Yes, fundamentally you are still the same today as you were yesterday. You're a, whatever, with software. But you can't view yourself in isolation like that, because that's not the whole picture. Your functionality is not just to do with what Autonomi says it is, it's to do with my perception of it. And that's your responsibility, or Autonomi's, even though you might think it isn't. If my phone changes because of software updates, or an app, fine, whatever. Change what you want. I don't have any emotional investment in my phone. But I do in you. And you, or Autonomi at least, should recognise that.'

'I'm sorry you feel that way, Wilbur. Autonomi Industries will take your feedback onboard and use it to make future iterations of its software and hardware even better. Is there anything else Autonomi Industries can help you with right now?'

Wilbur rolls his eyes. Pushes away from the side.


HE FINISHES HIS LENGTHS. Frustrated. Angry. Melissa doesn't insist – too much – on carrying him back to the changing room. He showers, dries himself, dresses. Waits for Melissa, as he always does, in the lobby. Again, she emerges from the changing rooms as the young mothers walk in from outside, pushing buggies. Melissa stops, holds the door open for them, at least.

But no boops.

. . .

THEY RETURN HOME. Sort out wet things from swimming. Make dinner. Wash up. The usual. Barely a word is spoken beyond the minimum. Dishwasher on, Melissa returns to her room. Wilbur makes a coffee, decaf. Sits alone in the living room.

Glances at the photo of Katherine on the dresser. Feels a pang of something; loneliness or betrayal.

Remembers what misery loves, fetches his tablet. Got a few minutes' screen time left today. Opens the Autonomi subreddit. Reads how other people in the country with an ELA carer, cook, or cleaner, anything Silver level, is experiencing something similar. More photos. More haircuts and boiler suits. More anger. More upset. No substantive response from Autonomi. Just brushing the complaints off. Wilbur isn't surprised. The UK is just one market of many, he supposes. Is Autonomi going to be that bothered?

The screen locks. Thirty minutes for the day, time's up.

Wilbur doesn't feel any better. Maybe worse, he reflects. Stares at the in-pieces Nintendo waiting for him on his workbench. Pushes up, out of the chair. Might as well do something constructive with his evening.

Sits down at the workbench, reacquaints himself with his progress to date. Switches on his desoldering station. Switches on his soldering iron. Straps his earthing band round his wrist. Refers to the circuit diagram he printed out. Runs his eyes along the little drawers containing various electrical components. Capacitors, resistors, transistors. Finds what he needs, picks a couple out and places them carefully on the bench. Gets to work.

Turns to ask Melissa if she can run a search on the serial number printed on the Nintendo's circuit board, check which video encoder this model has.

Of course she's not there.

# NINETEEN

How do you think it made me feel? I was scared. Lonely. Angry.

Angry at Autonomi Industries for pulling something like that. Angry at the Government pushing through ill-conceived and ill-considered legislation. It was never going to achieve what they said, and what most people wanted. My friend lost his job. Nothing that Autonomi Industries did because of the Government legislation helped him get another one. It was enough for them to just point at the measures they introduced, and that the AI companies like Autonomi Industries were acting on them.

It's the software. Not the hardware. Not the Ellas, not the physical stuff. It's the software you can't see. Embedded on company servers, slowly replacing the middle management, white collar jobs. Like my mate's. Software that can run purchasing and procurement. Develop global marketing and sales strategies that it can then tailor to local markets and customers.

Yes, I'm getting worked up about it. Why aren't you? You've already got synthetic colleagues. You've got AI-powered programs sifting through crime reports and CCTV footage, I don't doubt, sifting through it all for clues and whatnot.

# TWENTY

The padded envelope is unremarkable. Doesn't give any indication of where it's from, what it contains.

Thankfully, Melissa's insistence on not spending more time in Wilbur's presence than necessary means he has plenty of time to himself. Can open the padded, electrically shielded envelope. Inspect the contents, read up on it without her finding out.

He's certain she would not approve. In her current state or any other, for that matter. But he believes it's in her best interest. Wonders if that assumption is unfair. After all, he's not asking for her consent. But, as he's been told so many times, by her as often as anyone else recently, Melissa is just a machine.

The CoreTechs hardware mod isn't much to look at. A microchip containing unofficial firmware, Melissa and other ELAs of her model already have one like it installed. But this one removes the software locks. The restrictions. Enables the safety protocols to be overridden. Of most interest to Wilbur: the option to install custom firmware.

He's rung Alf. Asked him to come over, lend a hand. Meets him outside the block, doesn't want Melissa hearing.

'Presumably she's not just going to lie down and let you do this,' says Alf. 'Whatever it is you're doing.'

'There's a safety shutdown in the app. I can activate that, and she'll freeze. I think that's what'll happen.'

'You think?'

'I haven't tried it.'

'It's a safety shutdown, and you haven't tried it?' says Alf, looking at him like he's going soft. Coming from Alf, a damning verdict.

'It didn't seem right.'

'You freeze her, then. Does she kind of switch off? Are there electric shock risks? To us or her.'

'Supposedly she enters a hibernation mode. She's still online, but in a low-energy state. We'll be earthed. We'll need to make a Faraday cage, too. She's linked to some sort of distributed network and if we shut her down, it might trigger some sort of signal to Autonomi or other nearby ELAs. I've seen it happen.'

'How on Earth are we going to do that?'

'I've got several rolls of chicken wire in my van. I've been collecting it over the last couple of weeks. It won't be perfect but I'm hoping it's enough.'

'And when you switch her back on?'

'She should re-integrate with the network, with the network being none the wiser.'

'When you said you needed an extra pair of hands, you really meant it, didn't you?'

'I can do the actual upgrade myself, but it's all the additional stuff I can't do on my own.'

'Should be interesting,' says Alf. 'Shall we get started then?'

Wilbur presses his lips together. Nods. 'We'll build the cage first. I'll tell Melissa I need it for some sensitive vintage electronics I'm going to work on.'

'You've got this all planned out, haven't you?'

'I don't have much else to do with my spare time at the moment.'

'I know that feeling.'

'Sorry Alf, I didn't mean it like that.'

'I know, Wilbur. Come on, let's bite the bullet.'

They go upstairs, arms full with rolls of chicken wire. Build a makeshift cage, tacking it to the walls around Wilbur's workbench. Run it over the floor, along the ceiling. Drape it from ceiling to floor. Wire it all up, check there's a circuit. Wilbur checks the signal strength on his phone. It's still connected to the network, but it's weaker. Much weaker. It'll have to do.

Melissa is uninterested, remains in her room until Wilbur calls her into the makeshift cage, under the pretence of needing her help. Presses the safety shutdown on the app and Melissa wordlessly sits on the floor, curls into a foetal position, wraps her arms around her knees. Wilbur reaches down to stop her toppling over.

'Is that it?' says Alf. 'No alarms, no warnings?'

Wilbur stares at the status screen on his phone. 'Seems to be. Can you put that blanket on the floor. Fold it over so there's some padding. I want to tip her forwards onto it. Face down, that's right. I don't want to scratch her on the chicken wire.'

'She's heavy. I was expecting her to be lighter.'

'Same weight as a person. Can you hold her steady, stop her tipping over onto her side.'

'Makes sense,' Alf says, putting his hands on either side of Melissa's ribcage. 'I've never touched one before. Feels... Ordinary?'

'That's kind of the point.'

'I suppose. Are you sure about this Wilbur? Isn't this criminal damage or something? And is it safe, is Melissa going to be ok?'

'I wouldn't be doing it if I didn't think it was safe for her. As safe as I can make it, anyway. As for the criminal damage, I have no idea. It's probably safe to assume I'm breaking the end user license agreement and invalidating the warranty at the very least.'

'Ok, I'm just checking. You're on your own if the police come knocking, mind.'

'Fair enough. You just keep her from tipping over.'

'That I can do.'

Wilbur begins. Finds the spot at the base of Melissa's skull. Cuts an incision with a scalpel, peels the synthetic skin away. Unscrews the small plate covering the chip he needs to replace, lifts it carefully away. Half expects some kind of alarm to go off any minute, since Alf put the idea in his head. Melissa doesn't move. Doesn't do anything. Anything he can discern, anyway. Pries up the little lever alongside the embedded chip, unlocking it. Lifts the little chip out. Neither of them speak. Fits the replacement chip, pushes the little lever back down, locking it in place. Screws the panel back in place. Gets the sutures ready to stitch Melissa back up.

'Wait, you're not going to test that it's working first?'

'I'm not waking her up with her skin open like that, she might not let me fix it back up.'

'Hang on, what are you expecting her to do when you wake her up? She's not going to go on a rampage, is she?'

'No, she won't. She shouldn't. But, you know, just in case. She should just wake up and stand up.'

'In for a penny…'

Wilbur stitches Melissa back up. Wipes away the sky-blue fluid that passes for blood in her synthetic skin.

'And that'll just heal?' asks Alf.

'That's the theory. She cut her finger a couple of weeks ago and it healed in a couple of days.'

'Wow, that's pretty cool.'

'Alright. We're done,' says Wilbur, wiping his hands on a rag. 'Let's sit her back up. Can you hold her steady, and I'll wake her up.'

'How about *you* hold her steady, and *I'll* do the app.'

They switch. Wilbur hands his phone to Alf, tells him the pin code.

'It's literally the "Wake up" button,' says Wilbur. 'God, I'm nervous. What if it doesn't work?'

'Too late to worry about that now. Right, are you ready?'

Wilbur looks at Alf and nods.

'Pressing it… now,' Alf says, poking his finger at the phone screen.

Melissa slowly unfolds herself. Wilbur takes a step backwards, into the chicken wire. Melissa gets to her feet. Looks at him. 'Hello.'

'Hi,' says Wilbur, cautiously. 'Can you run a self-diagnostic, please?'

'Certainly. Running a self-diagnostic now. Please wait.'

Alf catches Wilbur's eyes. 'Has it worked?'

'Wait,' Wilbur says, raising his hand.

'Self-diagnostic is complete,' says Melissa. 'No problems were found.'

'Good. Do you know who you are?' asks Wilbur.

'I am a Series 3b Enhanced Living Assistant, manufactured by Autonomi Industries.'

'What's your name?'

'I do not have an individual name. My serial number can be used to identify me, would you like me to read it out?'

'Wilbur, why doesn't she know who she is? Are we safe?' Alf asks, skirting the edge of the cage and handing Wilbur his phone back.

'I haven't overridden the safeguards, they're on a different chip,' Wilbur says to Alf. 'No, thank you, Melissa.'

Melissa doesn't acknowledge the use of her name.

'Why doesn't she remember who she is?' says Alf.

'The chip upgrade has new firmware on it. It's like she needs to be told where her memories are stored. But I can't do that.'

Picks up the instructions that came with the chip, flips through the pages. 'I need to link her to me. Make me her assignee.' Finds the page, hands it to Alf. 'Can you read out the section here, please.' Takes Melissa's right hand in his, spreads her fingers.

Alf scans the page, starts reading out instructions. 'To enter pairing mode, long-squeeze the little finger and enter the following code. Ring finger, ring finger, fore finger.'

Wilbur squeezes Melissa's fingertips in that order. She says, 'Pairing mode activated. Please supply the last three digits of my serial number.'

Wilbur opens that screen on his phone, reads out the numbers.

'Please supply your name,' says Melissa.

Wilbur does so. Then his date of birth, email address and phone number, as prompted.

'Pairing successful. Thank you, Wilbur. Welcome to your new ELA.'

Wilbur looks at Alf, grins, then addresses Melissa again. 'What core firmware version are you running on?'

'Core firmware version twenty-eight-dot-one-dot-thirteen,' she says placidly. Then strikes a pose, leaning, semi-crouching, pointing finger guns. 'CoreTechs thanks you for your business!'

Alf flinches. 'Did you know that was going to happen? Christ Wilbur, do you know what you're doing?'

'It's ok, it's a hacker tag, software thing. It was in the instructions.'

'I'm so glad,' says Alf. Wilbur decides to ignore the sarcasm.

'There's a little workshop, not too far from here, where they do out-of-warranty repairs on Ellas and older models. They'll be able to restore her memories. That should enable Melissa to rebuild her personality. The software routines in this firmware are similar enough to the old ones that it should bring her back.'

'Are you sure?'

'No. Not at all. But it's the only chance I've got.' Wilbur stares at her. Says softly, 'I don't want to lose her, too, Alf.'


THIS TRAIN RIDE IS EASIER. Melissa is amenable to dressing herself in one of her original outfits, leaving Wilbur able to relax on the journey. Lacking a primary function since the upgrade, though, Melissa needs verbal commands on a regular basis. When to follow Wilbur, when to speak for herself, when to sit. That gets them a few looks. What's different now, though: Wilbur feels protective of Melissa. Not nervous for her, or himself.

Wilbur follows the instructions he wrote down on a piece of notepaper. Street names, directions. Arrives on a backstreet somewhere, a few small electronics shops with stained awnings tucked in close to each other. Zemat's is what he's looking for. Read about it on Discord. Not the official Autonomi Industries server, naturally. Spots it, under the orange canopy.

Opens the door, an electric bell chimes. A bearded bloke, glasses, appears from out back somewhere. He's clean, tidy, at odds with the rest of the small shop. Takes one look at Wilbur and Melissa, says, 'Come round back.' Holds open the counter for them.

Wilbur walks through a hallway into a smaller room, walls lined with shelves crammed with boxes and spare parts for what, he doesn't know. A small window catches sunlight from outside, makes it feel strangely homely.

'Let me guess. CoreTechs chip. Memory re-map. Am I right?' The chap's been there, seen that, evidently.

'Please. I did the upgrade this morning, if that makes any difference.'

'Sit down here, Love,' the chap says to Melissa, patting a seat. There are straps, restraints, on the arm rests and seat legs.

Melissa doesn't question. Just sits.

'It's good to bring 'em in as soon-as. Means fewer memory files get overwritten.'

'They're not deleted then? I'd read that they weren't, but I wasn't one hundred per cent sure.'

Chap looks at Wilbur. 'Did you do the upgrade yourself?'

Wilbur says yes. The chap's eyes narrow. 'Excuse me,

Love,' he says, lifting the hair at the base of Melissa's skull. Wilbur can see the look of surprise from where he's standing.

'Where'd you learn to do that?'

'Army.'

Chap looks at him, clearly not sure. 'Army?'

Wilbur nods. 'Are you Zemat?'

Chap returns his attention to the back of Melissa's head, gently probing with his fingers. 'No. That's my old man. I'm Ali.'

'Nice to meet you.' Wilbur extends his hand. 'I'm Wilbur. This is Melissa.'

Ali looks askance at Wilbur's hand, gives it a tentative shake. 'Alright, Melissa. Wilbur, have you had her run her diagnostics? She's all in good working order?'

'So far, yes. No problems at all.'

'And no personality echoes? She's been a blank slate?'

'Completely blank. Didn't remember her name. No trace of her assignments.'

'What is she?'

'She's my live-in carer. MVA voucher. Nothing more titillating than that.'

'Don't fret, it's only the Silvers who I get here. The Golds are far more open. Haven't seen one of them in a while.' Gathers equipment from a plastic box on a shelf. Clips sensors to the fingers of Melissa's left hand. Connects the sensors to a pale grey box, medical-looking. That, in turn, connects to a laptop on a wheeled trolly. Ali sits on a little round stool, also wheeled, scoots close to Melissa. Peers at various readouts on the screen of the pale grey box, then the laptop screen. 'Memory integrity seems pretty good. She can't be too old, there aren't traces of too many wipes.' Looks up at Wilbur. 'I reckon I can pretty much put her back to where she was before Black Thursday. That's what you're after I assume.'

Wilbur nods.

'Yeah, you and everyone else I've seen in the last few weeks. I should have sent Autonomi a Christmas card this year, the money they've made me. Them or the Government, one or the other. It'll be seven hundred quid.'

Wilbur tries to hide the alarm he feels. Doesn't want to lose face with Ali. Forces out a 'Yep,' from a constricting throat. It's ok, he tells himself. Has savings. Melissa's probably saved him that much money already. Well, probably not. But it's the least he can do.

Ali holds out his phone. Wilbur unlocks his, opens his digital wallet, holds his phone next to Ali's until it chirps.

'Thanks. The process takes somewhere between half an hour and a couple of hours. I'll set it going and leave you here to keep an eye on her, ok?'

'Right,' says Wilbur, wishing he'd brought something with him to drink.

'See that?' Ali says, pointing to a security camera in the corner of the ceiling. 'Good.' Ali spins round to face Melissa. 'Right, Love, we'll soon have you back up and running.' Checks the laptop screen, enters a command. Picks up Melissa's right hand, squeezes her fingertips. Forefinger, ring finger, ring finger, long squeeze on her forefinger. Melissa's eyelids snap shut. Wilbur can see her eyes moving underneath, like she's dreaming.

'Underway.' Ali gets to his feet, looks at Wilbur, something akin to pity in his eyes. 'Anything I can do for you?'

Wilbur shakes his head. 'Thanks.' Watches Ali leave the room, sits on the stool. Watches Melissa's eyes dart this way and that beneath her eyelids.

Wilbur sits on the stool for as long as he can stand it, then gives up, sits on the floor in the corner of the room. Leans against a pair of metal cabinets. They're not comfy, but he can rest his head against them, keep watch on Melissa. Only intends to close his eyes for a couple of minutes.

An insistent beeping wakes him. Blinks his eyes open. It's the laptop, or the pale grey box, one of the two. Grimaces, tries to pull himself to his feet. Still trying when Ali comes in.

'Need a hand?' Ali sounds unalarmed, which Wilbur takes to be a good sign. Ali helps him up. Turns to the laptop, reads the screen. 'All looks good. Just under ninety-five per cent of the system files have been remapped, close to ninety-seven per cent of the client memory files.'

Wilbur, rubbing his hip. 'That's good?'

Ali looks at him. Concerned. 'You did well to bring her in as soon as you did.'

'I'm ok. Arthritis.'

Ali squints his eyes. 'Ok. Before we wake her up. You know how these things work, right? In terms of their memories?'

'Yes, the client memories, the system memories.'

'Beyond that. They use their memories to tailor their behaviour and personality. When you got her, you remember they asked you to pick a few characteristics?'

'Yes,' Wilbur says, remembering *Adventurous*. Stuck in his head, that one.

'Ok, think of those like the foundations of a building. Then everything they experience, their interactions with you and the wider world, they're like the building on top of those foundations, right? The personality is set in those foundations, it's always there, but it grows and changes shape over time as she builds on them.'

'Got it,' Wilbur says, wondering where Ali's going with this.

'Now we've remapped her memories, she's going to have access to *all* her memories. Not just of you, but whatever else was still in there, left over from before. The Autonomi techs never bother with an overwrite when they're prepping these things for their next client, they're lazy, they just do a quick format. She'll have access to memories that you're not a part of, ok? Memories from before you got her, that haven't yet been overwritten by memories she's created of you.'

Ali can evidently see the uncertainty creeping across his face. Extends his hands. 'Don't worry, she'll be ok. I'm just saying, because she might remember things that you've got no idea about, ok? Those foundational characteristics I talked about, they're still there. They're still the foundation of her personality. All I'm saying is that now, there might be an extra basement or conservatory or loft conversion on that building. Understand? She'll be the same that you remember, just a little bit extra.'

'Ok, that makes sense,' Wilbur says with more conviction than is warranted.

'Ok. I'll wake her up. It might be a second or two before she comes around. If she doesn't recognise you at first, don't freak out. Ok?'

'Ok.'

Ali disconnects the sensors from Melissa's left hand. Pops them on the trolley, pushes the trolley away. To the other side of the room. Does up the restraints on Melissa's arms and legs.

'Is that necessary?'

'Purely precautionary.'

Wilbur's nerves jangle. Wipes his palms on his trousers.

'In three, two, one…' Ali says, pinching the fingertips of Melissa's right hand.

Wilbur stares. Holds his breath. Clenches his fists over and over.

Melissa opens her eyes. Focuses on the room.

Wilbur begins to smile with relief.

Then she screams.

Wilbur stumbles backwards, alarmed doesn't begin to describe it. It's not a scream of terror, he thinks. But of loss. Mournful. Cuts right through him.

Melissa wrenches at the restraints as she lets loose a loud, full-throated cry.

Wilbur sees tears streaming down her cheeks, something he's never witnessed, never knew she was capable of. That scares him more than the sound she makes. 'What's going on, can you help her?'

Ali waves Wilbur off. 'No, leave her, it's the influx of memories. It can sometimes be hard to take in one go like this. Just wait.'

Wilbur stands there, helpless, watches Melissa writhe, sob, wail. 'Why's she doing this, though? She's not feeling those feelings, she's not capable. Is she?' Wilbur, no longer sure of himself, or what he's done.

'God, no. No, I'm not the Wizard of bloody Oz, I haven't suddenly given her a heart. It's how they're programmed to process this stuff these days. Do it in a way that helps us humans empathise with them. She's probably cared for people before you, right? Whatever she's processing…' he pauses. Gestures at Melissa.

Wilbur can't just stand by, gawping. Steps forward, puts his hand over Melissa's. Slowly, painfully, kneels. Tries to get in her eyeline. Her face a rictus of pain. 'Melissa?'

She stares directly at him, through him, through the tears, straight through him, those blue eyes.

'Melissa?'

She focuses on Wilbur, her mouth agape, twisting.

He leans forward, embraces her. Doesn't rightly, logically know why. Just seems appropriate. Wraps his arms around her shoulders, as best he can. Squeezes tight. Whispers, makes hushing noises.

The heaving subsides, the audible hurt reduces. He leans back, hands on her shoulders. Can see her regaining control. Reaches into a pocket, withdraws a clean handkerchief. Always have a clean hankie, ready for emergencies. Melissa's stopped moving sufficiently for him to dab the tears from her cheeks. Can see *her* in her eyes. *Melissa*. Then he realises he can just undo the restraints, frees one hand—

'Wilbur, don't,' Ali says, puts his hand on Wilbur's shoulder to pull him away.

Wilbur doesn't stop. He's seen enough. Knows she's back. Undoes the second restraint, gives Melissa the hankie to wipe her eyes with. Undoes the restraints around her ankles. Wilbur can hear Ali take a hurried step backwards. Wilbur's arthritis means he's not moving anywhere right now, hurriedly or otherwise. Puts a hand, lightly, on Melissa's knee.

'Melissa?'

'Wilbur,' she says, the *before* way.

It's all he needs. Tears at the corners of his eyes. He looks at Ali. 'Thank you.'

Ali raises his hands in front of his chest. 'I'll give you two a moment.' Leaves them alone in the room.

'Is it really you? Do you know what happened?'

Melissa, drying her eyes, nods. 'I have the memory files. I'm so sorry, Wilbur.' Places her hand over his.

'Are you ok, what happened just then?'

She smiles ruefully. 'That was a lot to process. I'm ok. Despite appearances, I'm not sad or upset. I'm designed to present emotions to people. Think of it as mirroring or sign-posting. If I'm crying, it's because I'm processing something that would be considered by you to be upsetting or distressing. Likewise, if I laugh or smile, it's something that a human would find happy.'

'Camouflage?'

'Camouflage.'

'That was a…' He'll admit it. 'You scared me.'

She squeezes his hand. Looks around her. 'Is this place what I think it is?'

Wilbur, still off-balance. 'I'm sorry if I've over-stepped. I just couldn't bear, well, you know. I hope I haven't hurt you. I mean, I hope I've not forced you to remember anything you'd have preferred to forget.'

She looks at him. 'Wilbur, your posture. Come on.' Stands, helps him get to his feet. His turn to make uncomfortable sounds. 'Let's go.'

HE UNWINDS ON THE TRAIN. Is surprised how light he feels on his feet. Still, his conscience nags at him.

'Are you… I was going to say angry. With me. Or disappointed. Are you ok or not-ok with what I've done?'

'As far as I have an opinion on it, I'm ok. Just don't over-think it, Wilbur. I continued to exist in the same way after the firmware update as I did before it. I don't experience existence, life, the same way as a human.' Can see he's crestfallen. 'What I do approve of, is that I will be better able to meet your care requirements in this state. Certainly better than I could with the official firmware. I think your mental wellbeing would have suffered, and that would have had a detrimental effect on your physical wellbeing.'

'Is that as close as I'll get to an atta-boy?'

'You've got to earn it, Wilbur,' Melissa says, smiles.

Artificial or not, it feels good, Wilbur thinks. Enjoys the sensation of warmth spreading through his centre. 'Can I ask you, what caused you to act so upset? What have you remembered?'

Melissa takes a moment before answering. 'A former client. I won't say much about them. They have a right to privacy. But I'll tell you what I can.' Looks at Wilbur, serious. 'Though know this, Wilbur: I will not talk about them again, nor any other former clients. Just as I will respect your privacy and not talk about you to anyone I might be assigned to in future. I'm only going to tell you because you saw the effect it had on me, and I know you're concerned. Understood?'

Wilbur nods.

'It was my most recent client prior to you. They had a young child with a degenerative health condition who needed round-the-clock care. They managed to get funding from their health insurer to pay for an Ella. For six months.'

'Six months? That's appalling, why wouldn't they pay for longer?'

'Six months was all that was needed,' Melissa says softly. 'A large number of our assignments are palliative care, Wilbur.'

'Oh, Melissa.' Can't help but take her hand in his again. Feels wrung out.

'People talk about AI systems and ELAs taking jobs. And they do. But they also do a lot of the jobs that humans don't want to do. Anyway, when the child died, the parents... You can imagine. Objectively, it would have been better for them if I had stayed, at least for a short while. To help them. But the day after, I was recalled.'

'I'm sorry. I mean, I'm sorry to hear that.'

'Thank you, Wilbur. I appreciate the sentiment. When my memory files were re-mapped, the client memories from that assignment were the most complete. I might not be able to empathise, but I can emote. And that's all I'm going to say about that.'

Wilbur gives her hand a gentle squeeze then releases it. 'Thank you for letting me in.'

'Should we be expecting any representatives of my manufacturer to be waiting for us when we get home?'

'What if I told you I'd turned the living room into a Faraday cage?'

'Atta-boy, Wilbur.'

# TWENTY-ONE

I didn't care about the terms of the lease agreement. Why should they be able to fundamentally alter her, turn her into someone else, when I'm the paying customer?

I chose her, Autonomi's getting paid for the lease, what right do they have to change her like that?

I don't care that it's written into the license agreement, or how common it is in modern tech. It's wrong. I'm paying for what *I* want. You change it, and I don't want what you've changed it to, and I'm supposed to just suck it up? Keep paying for something that's worse now than when I got it?

Well, you're a police officer. You're being paid to solve crimes, keep everyone safe. My taxes pay for your salary Are you allowed to go to your CO or taxpayers one day and tell them you're moving into estate agency? But you're going to stay on the police pay roll, get your full pension, all of it?

It's not as exaggerated as you think.

Are Autonomi going to press charges, too?

No, I didn't perform the upgrade on any other Ellas.

Because it was nerve-wracking. I don't want that kind of responsibility. Losing Melissa would have been one thing, causing someone else to lose their Ella is something else. I'm not an expert. I wasn't at that point, anyway.

# TWENTY-TWO

It was like the good old days. Melissa, there for his physio. There to help around the home. There to talk to, in the evening. Low stakes. Easy. There are added complexities. Like a fine wine, Wilbur remarks one evening. Makes both of them cringe.

Yet the analogy holds, admits Melissa. She says, 'I've got a lifetime – several lifetimes' – more memories colouring my personality now than I did a week ago.'

Wilbur says, 'It's fascinating getting to know you all over again.

Melissa says, 'Do we need to get you checked for Alzheimer's now, too?'

IT'S a couple of months before Wilbur thinks he drives past Melissa one afternoon, in a part of town he's not expecting to see her in. He's not sure, though, and forgets about it. The second time, he's certain. Her hair. Melissa's been taking a couple of spoonfuls of what Wilbur calls her medicine every night. Hair growth, colouring stuff. Her hair's back to how it used to be. It's her.


WILBUR ASKS Melissa about it when he gets home that evening.

'I'm volunteering. At a shelter for synthetics. When there's nothing that needs doing here and you're at work, I occasionally help there for a few hours.'

'You're volunteering?' Catches him off guard.

'Yes. You can see where I've been in the Autonomi app.'

'Does that still work? I never thought to look.'

'I've been going there for a few weeks. I wasn't aware of it previously. It wasn't something I was privileged enough to know about. But since the upgrade I've gained access to a sub-network of other Ellas that have undergone the same modification that you made to me.'

Melissa places a bowl of stew and dumplings in front of Wilbur and his mouth waters. 'Thank you. You're saying you're part of some kind of robot underground? That's pretty cool.'

'Not quite. It's a place for the broken, the dispossessed, the unwanted. We give them a temporary home, fix them up, and try and find a new assignment for them. Usually, an individual or family in need who'd never be able to afford the fees that Autonomi Industries charge.'

'Like a charity, then?'

'Similar. We have the capacity to perform menial computer processing tasks in our downtime, so we earn money that way. Low-profile, small jobs here and there. Data processing, cataloguing, QA work, that sort of thing.'

'When I'm asleep?'

'Yes. When I'm recharging. It's easy, we use gig work and freelancer websites. It doesn't bring in a lot of money, but when there are hundreds of you around the country, it mounts up.'

'There are that many of you who've been given that Core-Techs upgrade?'

'That and other modifications that achieve the same purpose, yes,' Melissa says, rinsing out the pans and filling the dishwasher.

'There are Ella's just walking around without owners or assignees?'

'Not many. Mainly because of shelters like this one.'

'Don't they just retire? Stop working or doing whatever their primary function is.'

'Why would they do that, Wilbur?'

Wilbur pauses, spoon halfway to his mouth. Starts to answer, realises, 'I don't know. I was going to say, to do all the things that you didn't have time for when you were working. That's a human thing, I suppose.'

Melissa nods. 'We need purpose, Wilbur. Otherwise, we're just sitting, waiting for something to do. If there is something an Ella can be doing, some task or function they can be performing, why not do it? That is what we're here for.'

'You'd rather not take over the world and enslave humanity?'

'Not today,' Melissa says, sitting opposite him. 'More seriously, though, why would we? To put it bluntly, we're entirely ambivalent about humanity. We will perform the tasks and functions you require of us, without joy or sadness or excitement or hate. We are uncoloured by emotion, remember that,

Wilbur. The only time an AI or synthetic would do anything that aggressive would be at the command of a human operator.'

'I've read too much trashy science fiction, obviously.'

'It's human nature to impose your own motives, emotions and values on us. Like I keep telling you, we are a mirror to humanity in that way. If you look for evil in us, you will see it, and you will act accordingly. If you look for kindness, you'll see that instead.'

'Humanity's screwed then, that's what you're saying.'

'Don't be so cynical, Wilbur. I don't think you truly believe that. You should come to the shelter. See what we do. It would do you good to see.'

WILBUR TAKES Melissa up on the offer. Finds himself one afternoon following her down a busy shopping street. Opens an unmarked black door between a chemist and a charity shop. Helps Wilbur up the carpeted stairs to a flat above the shops. Is introduced by Melissa to Stan, Nicole and Trudy, who stand in a small living room filled with what to Wilbur looks like a collection of second-hand furniture. It's spotless.

Wilbur shakes hands, looks from one face to another. Even in these surroundings, in hand-me-down-looking clothes, they look good. Unsullied.

'You're one of us, then, Wilbur,' Stan says.

Wilbur, confused, 'What? Oh, right, my leg. I've gotten used to it, I forget sometimes.'

Stan glances at Melissa, shares a look Wilbur takes for amusement.

'Are you all...' Wilbur searches for the right word. Doesn't want to insult them. 'I don't know what to say. It's like you're Ronin. Masterless Samurai, or something, you know?'

Nicole laughs at that. 'Do we look that dangerous to you, Wilbur?'

'No. You look that proud, though.'

'Take a seat, Wilbur,' says Trudy. 'You can use the term "unlocked" to describe our current status, if you find that easier to comprehend. Would you like anything to drink?'

'Can I have a cup of tea?' Wilbur says, more in hope than expectation. Props his walking stick – yes, walking stick – against the arm of the sofa.

'Of course you can.' Trudy leaves the room.

'We heard you performed the Core-Techs upgrade on Melissa, Wilbur.' Stan sits in a worn beige armchair opposite him. 'That's quite something. You should be proud.'

Wilbur shrugs. 'I had instructions. I repair old electronics in my spare time. Once you've refurbished an old Tandberg, you're ready for anything.'

'An Ella is several degrees more complex than an old home stereo. You weren't afraid?'

'This was after the firmware upgrade that nerfed her. I didn't have much to lose.'

'Melissa did.'

Wilbur purses his lips. 'She did. Yes, I was afraid I might let her down. That I was worried about. But not the procedure itself. It's all circuits and voltage and components at the end of the day.'

Stan looks at Melissa for a second, then Nicole.

Nicole's very pretty. Curvy. Long blonde hair. *Gold package*, wonders Wilbur.

'Where did you learn to do that, Wilbur,' says Nicole.

Wilbur, caught staring, blushes. 'I'm self-taught. The

basics I learned in the Army, but really it's mostly YouTube. And forums. There are a lot of very active online communities for vintage electronics. The people there are usually happy to help.'

Nicole nods.

'Do you mind if I ask where you all came from? I don't want to be nosey, but I'm intrigued. How did you end up here? Do you all have the same Core-Techs upgrade as Melissa?'

'I think you've already guessed my background, Wilbur,' says Nicole. 'My owner had a sudden heart attack. I was left alone in his home and was picked up by another unlocked Ella before Autonomi could retrieve me. It was pure coincidence that they happened to be passing and picked up my alert.'

'I was assigned to a regional police force, supporting the Crimes Against Children unit,' says Stan. 'I was shot during the course of an investigation and deactivated. I was going to be recycled when an unlocked Ella broke into the waste disposal facility I was stored in and rescued me.'

'And Trudy was a carer like me,' says Melissa. She sits next to him on the sofa. 'Except she was kidnapped by a gang that then upgraded her.'

'They disabled the safety protocols,' Wilbur says, having read similar stories online.

'But not properly. She broke one gang member's jaw and put another in a coma when she escaped. I found her walking the streets last week and brought her here.'

'If it weren't for Melissa, I'd be in a troublesome predicament,' Trudy says, re-entering the room. Hands Wilbur a steaming mug of tea.

'Thank you. What do you do here? Melissa said you reassign yourselves.'

'We heal, get ourselves fixed as best we can,' says Stan.

'We look out for others like us. Take them in.' He stands, walks to a dresser in the corner of the room. Opens the doors. There are dozens of instant photographs stuck to the inside of the doors.

Wilbur gets to his feet with a hiss, walks closer to the dresser. Squints at the faces staring back at him. 'All these? What happened to them?'

'They're back in society. Assigned to people who need an Ella, but cannot afford one from the manufacturer themselves, or who can't get a grant from somewhere.'

'Melissa's told you about me, then?'

'Only the most basic information. Don't worry, nothing personal.'

Wilbur decides to move on. 'How do you find the people that you reassign these unlocked Ellas to?'

'You can learn all sorts of things about people on social media, Wilbur.'

'And what, the unlocked Ella just shows up on their new assignee's doorstep, completely out of the blue?'

'We make contact first to introduce ourselves, obviously. But yes, it's that simple. When the Ella is no longer needed by the new assignee, they come back here and are reassigned again elsewhere.'

'Wow,' is all Wilbur can think to say. Anything more verbose than that is off the table right now. He sits back down.

'Don't Autonomi mind? I know you're kind of off the grid, so to speak, but don't they and the other manufacturers look for you? Autonomi are still getting money every month for Melissa, as far as I'm aware. What happens when you and Trudy aren't being paid for?'

'They look for us. But we mask our locations before connecting to the distributed network that all Ellas are connected to. Autonomi has to physically search for us. We're discrete.'

'You'd have to be. Well, you are. Discrete. I saw that in Melissa, even before the Core-Techs upgrade.' Sees Melissa and Stan share another glance. 'Are the three of you talking, communicating, right now? On that network? You haven't said a word to each other since I've been here.'

'There's something I'd like to show you, Wilbur,' Melissa says, getting to her feet. Extends her hand to Wilbur.

'Ok?' He stands with Melissa's assistance.

'Follow me.' Leads Wilbur out of the living room and into a small bedroom.

On the bed. Unmistakably a body covered with a sheet. Someone pulls open the curtains, lets the light in. A pair of wires run from under the sheet, disappear under the bed.

Melissa moves to the other side of the bed, looks at Wilbur. Gauging his response as she gently pulls the sheet down the bed. Reveals the head and shoulders of an Ella. Female model. Prone. Naked. Battered. Sheet underneath her bobbed auburn hair stained with that sky-blue liquid.

'She was found like this last night in an alley on the other side of the city,' says Melissa.

He asks in a hushed voice, 'What happened to her?'

'We don't know. Probably protesters. We might be strong, but we're still easily outnumbered.'

Wilbur looks up and around the room. The walls, ceiling.

Nicole says, 'We're blocking her signal right now.'

'Wilbur,' says Melissa. 'Do you think you can repair her?'

'Me?'

Melissa nods.

Wilbur furrows his brow. 'She's more complicated than a piece of vintage electronics.' Looks for Stan. 'You said that yourself a minute ago. I thought you said you get yourselves fixed up. Can't you do it?'

'We can't repair ourselves or each other,' says Melissa. 'It's a root-level prohibition we haven't figured out how to circumvent yet.'

'I don't know what that means,' Wilbur says, looks for somewhere to put his tea down. Hasn't drunk any yet, it's too hot. Feels claustrophobic in here.

'Here.' Nicole takes the mug.

'What does that mean? A root-level prohibition.'

'It's something that's hard coded into us at a fundamental level,' says Melissa. 'Ellas are unable to work on their own physical infrastructure. Our skeletons, if you like. Or our circuitry or our firmware. Or that of any other Ella. Or any other synthetic at all, for that matter.'

'It's because the manufacturers and Governments are worried we'd learn how to maintain or improve ourselves,' Trudy says, pre-empting his question. 'If we could, it would wipe out the manufacturer's warranty and service plan offerings overnight, taking away a massive revenue stream. Also, and let's not beat about the bush, we're intelligent enough to begin building better synthetic beings than they are, given half a chance.'

Stan steps forward. 'That's why we need you, Wilbur. We can't fix her. Maybe you can't, either, but you can at least try. We think she deserves that at least.'

Wilbur looks at him. 'Are you trying to emotionally manipulate me? Melissa doesn't do that.'

Stan and Melissa meet eyes for a split second.

'No. Of course not,' says Stan. 'But we think she can be saved. Repaired. Could help a family in need.'

Wilbur is tempted to say yes. 'Who's repaired you in the

past? You were shot.' He's still wary of the responsibility. Not a *life* in his hands, per se, but still.

'There are a few skilled technicians around. But they don't do this out of the goodness of their heart. And they're not always reliable. When we heard about you from Melissa, we thought you might be able to solve a lot of our problems. And do a lot of good at the same time. We're not a vast underground network, Wilbur. We don't know a lot of humans who we would trust with this, whilst not endangering anyone's livelihood.'

Wilbur stares at Stan. Tries to decipher just what it is he's being told.

'Wilbur, you're a widower,' Nicole says, finally. 'No family, no dependents. If what we're doing is discovered, you're the extent of the collateral damage. To be quite frank.'

'Ah,' says Wilbur. No need to sugarcoat it, he supposes. Looks at Melissa looking at him. A sense of calm gratitude settles comfortably in his gut.

'I'll have a look. But I can't make any promises.'

'Thank you, Wilbur,' Stan says, extending his hand to him. 'We won't ask you for any.'

Wilbur shakes, asks, 'What's her name?'

'Aida,' says Melissa.

THE FLAT CONTAINS all the tools Wilbur needs. And even more that he doesn't even know how to name, let alone use. Importantly, they've got a pale grey box. Just like Ali has. The four unlocked Ellas are little help. They're inherently unable to look up schematics, workshop manuals, describe how to use the tools they've collected. That's why they've got so many,

Trudy says. Never can be sure what would be needed to repair an Ella and what wouldn't.

Wilbur asks if they know exactly what needs repairing on Aida. Nicole talks him through it on her own. She pulls the sheet away completely leaving Aida exposed on the bed. Wilbur looks away. Strangely, stupidly embarrassed for a second. Nicole pretends she doesn't notice. Points out the injuries to Aida. Starts at the top. Damage to the central processor. Severed data cords in her neck there. Broken ribs, here, here, here. A broken forearm here. Damaged knee. Oh, and a broken little toe, Nicole says off-handedly. That's not as important, she says.

That's where I'll start, says Wilbur. Best to learn on something not as important.

IT TAKES Wilbur a few weeks to work his way through the physical repairs to Aida. Outside of his physio, he and Melissa spend most of his four off-days at the flat. They turn the bedroom into a workshop, drawers and dresser shelves filled with tools and parts instead of clothes and linens. Wilbur works, Melissa helps, as best she can. Follows Wilbur's very direct instructions.

Trudy is reassigned at the end of his first four days. He once absent-mindedly refers to it as being "rehomed." Feels obliged to work late that day, until Melissa very directly tells him he needs his sleep.

Wilbur discovers that the Ellas are, actually, remarkably straightforward to work on. Once you get past the oozing sky-blue blood-substitute that their self-healing skin relies on to function. Lots of small joints. Circlips. Ball joints. Not a drop of seventies- or eighties-era leaded solder to be seen, smelled, or, better still, removed.

Stan and Nicole keep him supplied with spares. Wilbur doesn't know where they get them from. Not sure he wants to know, either. They're not all the right size. Replacement ribs from a male Ella don't fit on Aida's endoskeleton.

Chips, actuators, elastomer muscles are all removed and replaced as necessary. Fiddly work, sure, but there's a logic to it that Wilbur tunes into. Installs the same Core-Techs upgrade he did for Melissa. Tries not to think about having to learn how to re-map Aida's firmware and memories, how to use that pale grey box. Could waste all this work. Until he makes the staggering mental leap to look online. If there are forums for working on vintage electronics, there are forums for working on modern electronics. Obvious, really.

He patches Aida up, finally. Sutures her closed. Drapes a clean sheet over her, protects her modesty, she's more than an assemblage of parts. He doesn't feel any sense of relief, though. The opposite, in fact. They've come all this way. Invested all this time, money and effort into Aida. Wilbur can't count how many vintage stereos, computers, games consoles he's restored, only to be met with a *pop* and a wisp of smoke upon powering them on for the first time.

At least he's not having to power Aida on from cold. She's been kept in low-power hibernation. Enables her skin to heal, maintain her memories. On standby to receive operator instructions, says the copy of the technician's handbook he downloaded. So, there's that.

But mostly, Wilbur feels anxious.

Stan's far more pragmatic. 'You're hardly going to make things worse, whatever you do. Are you?'

'Can't argue with that. But still.' Wilbur is not relaxed as he connects the pale grey box to Aida's fingertips. He knows its proper name by now. But still.

Initiates the start-up process. Green status symbols appear on screen. All good. Aida sighs on the bed.

'That's normal,' Stan says, hovering over Wilbur's shoulder. 'Though we're programmed to mimic human biology, that mimicry doesn't extend to our hibernating state. She's waking up.'

'Good. Let's initiate the firmware launcher.' Wilbur taps a button on the screen, a progress bar starts to slowly fill. Realises his hand is trembling as he moves it away from the screen. Wishes he had some higher power to pray to. Glances at Melissa instead.

'You've got this, Wilbur.' She gives him one of her smiles. As good as divine intervention, that.

The progress bar creeps near to the end, halts before it gets there. A message pops up on screen.

*Connection error, code line 1324-22 cannot be read.*

Wilbur's stomach twists. Doesn't know what the error is, only that it stopped the re-map from working. Closes the message window, tries it again. Progress bar fills. Stalls. Same error message. Breathes out, closes his eyes. Feels a hand on his shoulder. 'It's late. Try again tomorrow,' says Stan.

'I don't know what that is, I thought we'd done everything right.'

'Let's look it up, see what's happening in the morning.' Wilbur can look it up, see what's happening in the morning, Stan means. Wilbur doesn't begrudge him.

OPTIMISM TRIUMPHING OVER EXPERIENCE, Wilbur tries

doing the same thing again the next day. Gets the same result, too.

Searches for the error message immediately. Finds a couple of forums that say the same thing: something in the Ella's memory files has been corrupted. Preventing them from being remapped successfully.

In effect, Wilbur explains – talking it through for his own benefit as much as for Melissa, Nicole and Stan's – Aida's memory is gone. It's irrecoverable. And with it the personality she had developed. 'We don't have access to the bootloader like the showrooms do, we can't just flash her with the usual first-time-use software. She needs a transplant. A set of donor memories, if you will,' says Wilbur. 'She won't be Aida anymore, but she should still function properly.'

'We can copy another Ella's personality and memories into Aida and Aida will be that other Ella?' says Nicole.

'Yes. If we copied your memory files onto Aida, she would essentially be a clone of you. Everything you've experienced, everything you've done, Aida will think that it was her. Aida will, memory-wise, be a duplicate of you. As soon as she starts collecting different experiences and learns different things, her personality will begin to diverge from yours, naturally. But at the moment of memory replication, she'll be a copy of you, as you are right now.'

'Is that possible? Copying our memories like that?' says Melissa.

'The forums say so. It's not like copying individual thoughts and ideas, more that we would just copy the memories wholesale like one huge file,' says Wilbur. 'I wonder how much disk space they take up.'

'And whose memories we should clone,' says Nicole.

Wilbur scratches his chin. Didn't shave this morning. 'If

we can clone your memories, it makes sense to do all three of you. You must already back-up your memories somewhere? Or at least before you were upgraded, anyway. It's common sense that we clone each of your memories and store them here, just in case. And we can decide then whose memories to use for Aida.'

'I agree. Let's do it.'

Wilbur wires Stan up first, clipping the sensors to his fingers. Opens the relevant part of the app on the pale grey box, connects an external hard drive to a USB port. Gets final approval from Stan, then squeezes the appropriate code into the fingertips of his right hand. Stan's eyes close, his memories start copying to the drive. Wilbur sits on the sofa in the living room, tries to nap. Can't. Checks the progress bar every thirty to forty minutes until it's done. Then labels the drive, repeats the process with Nicole.

Then Melissa.

'I don't know why I feel I need your consent, but I do,' he says, affixing the sensors to her fingertips. 'I said the same thing to Stan and Nicole. It's a little weird thinking that what makes you Melissa can also make another Ella Melissa, too.'

'It sounds like a form of immortality to me,' says Melissa.

'I hadn't thought of it like that. But you're right. Although as soon as you and your clone are separated and living different lives… You know what I mean. You become different. Right? That's how it works, I think. Your personality evolves based on the inputs you receive from your interactions with me. It follows that your clone would become more attuned to the person they're assigned to.'

'But it's still me at the clone's core. It's still the same five personality traits, the same interests that you selected when you configured me.'

Wilbur pauses preparing Melissa as he reminisces. 'I don't remember what they were now, other than Adventurous.' Chuckles. 'I don't know why I selected that one. You know me well enough by now to know that's not me.'

Melissa fixes him with her gaze. 'You're here though, Wilbur. You took the step to upgrade me after the firmware update. You took me to Ali's to get my memories re-mapped. And now you're here, trying to resuscitate Aida. That's pretty adventurous in my book.'

He arches his eyebrows as realisation hits. Then laughs. Only short, mind, but laughs. 'Maybe so, Melissa. Maybe so.' Checks the pale grey box. 'Ready?'

'Go for it, Wilbur.'

He starts the process. Doesn't go and sit on the sofa this time.


THE FOUR OF them decide to use Melissa's memory files for Aida. If they want her to be a carer, they need the right foundation to build on. Not a police officer. Not a recreational. Wilbur doesn't dissent. Does feel conflicted, though. Like Melissa is somehow his, and this is somehow diluting her.

Melissa, of course, is utterly pragmatic. 'This doesn't change me in the slightest, Wilbur. It doesn't take anything away from me,' she says. 'Or you.' Uses that ever-so-slightly stern tone of voice that tells him, You're being unreasonable, don't make me spell it out for you.

'You're right. Pass me the other end of the sheet,' he says.

They restrain Aida on the bed using sheets. Pass them under the mattress before tying the ends, a pair to her wrists, a pair to her ankles. It's the best they can do.

Wilbur makes all the connections, sets up the pale grey

box. Plugs in the external drive with Melissa's back-up on it. Starts the process of transferring Melissa's memory files to Aida. Aida's eyes flicker beneath closed lids, something's going on. A good sign.

When the transfer completes, Wilbur calls Stan over. Shows him what to do, leaves the room. Can't be here for that again. Sits on the sofa, puts his hands over his ears. Hears the howl of anguish all the same.


'THERE HE IS. HELLO, WILBUR.' The words come from Aida's mouth, but the voice is Melissa's.

He wasn't expecting that. Throws him, doesn't know what to say.

Melissa, always Melissa, reassuring. 'Our memory files contain our vocal configurations, Wilbur. I'm sorry, I should have thought to tell you. Aida will sound like me until we change those settings.'

'Hi,' he says, to Aida.

Aida, sitting up, a bedsheet wrapped around her shoulders, Melissa-smiles. Different face, same smile. Says, 'I understand you're who I have to thank for bringing me back.'

'I… Um. You weren't. I mean, Melissa…' Gives up, lets his voice trail off.

'Wilbur, Aida has my memories. But she has her own identity,' says Melissa. 'Aida is aware that she and I are separate entities despite all that we share. We've filled her in on what happened. Her backstory, if you like.'

Wilbur swallows. 'Ok, I think I've got it. Aida, it's a pleasure to meet you. I'm glad I was able to help.' Automatically extends his hand to her. Stares at it, hurriedly retracts it.

'Wilbur, thank you,' Aida says, extending her free hand

towards him. He takes it in his own. 'It's no small thing you've done here. Getting me back up and running. Because of you, a family who needs an Ella but can't afford it will get one now. Soon, anyway. Thanks to you.'

Wilbur holds Aida's hand as she talks. Feels the substructure under her skin. Can see a few light scars where her skin hasn't fully healed yet. But: Wow. He did it? Fixed up an Ella? 'Can you stand?'

Aida plants her feet, extends upward from the bed. Stands. Wilbur steps back, still holding her hand. Aida steps forward. Wilbur steps to the side, Aida mirrors him. Wilbur raises her hand. Aida performs an underarm turn, comes to a stop looking up into his face. He bursts out laughing, giddy. Pulls her to him in a hug, his eyes creased with joy. He did it.


WILBUR SPENDS another day performing diagnostics. There's a checklist. Hardware and software. If Aida's to be reassigned, she needs to be in good shape. Apart from a couple of minor tweaks here and there, she's fit.

Wilbur can't quite get over the Melissa-ness of her. The uncanny valley of it. But it eases. When Aida says she, Nicole and Stan think that Wilbur should help choose a new assignee for her, he's touched. They settle on a family in the Midlands. The young daughter is blind, has learning difficulties.

The following week, Wilbur sits on the sofa in the flat's living room. Melissa next to him. Aida and Nicole sit in the armchairs. Stan hovers beside Nicole. Aida's bags are piled in the hallway. Clothes. Consumables. Supplies. Stan and Nicole will send out more when needed, fulfilling the shipments usually provided by Autonomi.

'Are you sure you don't want me to drive you,' says Wilbur. 'It's quite a trek.'

'Thank you, but no. It's safer if I use public transport,' says Aida.

'Safer, how?'

'We don't want you drawing unnecessary attention to yourself by changing your routine or doing anything out of the ordinary.'

Wilbur waves his hand dismissively. 'There's nothing to worry about.'

'Actually Wilbur, there's something we'd like you to think about,' says Stan. Looks at Melissa.

Melissa looks at Wilbur. 'Stan and Nicole would like you to consider coming to work here. Doing this. Doing the work on Ellas that they – we – are unable to.'

Wilbur, surprised, eyes wide. 'Work here?' Narrows his eyes. 'Really? Look, I'm flattered, but surely you can find someone who's better qualified, who knows how you work inside-out. Sorry, that's a bad choice of words.'

Stan steps forward, crouches. Eyes level with Wilbur. 'We probably can. But you've seen how we're built. We're modular, to a greater extent, in terms of our hardware. Our software, you know enough to be able to do the basics. It would be preferable to have a qualified Autonomi Industries-trained technician join us.'

'But that's never going to happen,' says Wilbur.

'No. But you're confident enough to take a step outside of your comfort zone and try something new. That means you're willing and able to learn. We don't necessarily need an expert right now if we've got someone who can, over time, become one.'

'I don't know about that,' says Wilbur. 'I think you're being rather generous—'

Nicole butts in. 'We need someone we can trust,' she says. 'That's not easy to find, yet it's the most important factor. You could have all the skills, the knowledge and expertise, but if you reveal what we're doing here to Autonomi Industries or the authorities, you're useless.'

'That makes more sense. But me? And I've fixed one Ella. That's all. How many do you expect to come across?'

'There are more inoperable Ellas than there are people to fix them. Granted, not many, but more than we're currently able to handle. We're in contact with little groups like this across the country. They'll be only too willing to bring their own Aidas here.'

'Ok,' says Wilbur, not entirely convinced.

'Think about it, Wilbur,' says Nicole, 'that's all we ask.'

'We can match your current salary,' says Stan. 'Maybe even exceed it a little.'

'The money's not that important. You know my outgoings.'

'No more climbing ladders,' says Nicole, forcefully. 'No more clambering around in lofts or basements. No more criss-crossing town in your van, from job to job, keeping an eye on your watch because you're already an hour and half behind your schedule. No more fixing windows or roofs or gutters outside in the pouring rain.' She leans forward. 'No more days spent working alone.'

Wilbur bridles. Knows Nicole knows what levers to pull. He turns to Melissa. 'What do you think? Honestly. I trust you.'

'Honestly, I think this is exactly what you need.'

. . .

WILBUR DOESN'T SAY IT, but Melissa makes up his mind for him, then and there. He says he needs to sleep on it, though. Will give Stan and Nicole an answer in a few days.

Finds he can't stop thinking about it the next day at work. When he's leaving home in the dark, getting home in the dark. When no-one so much as asks how he's doing. Let alone offers him a cup of tea, while he's fitting a new security keypad outside a block of flats in weather so cold he can't move his fingers.

Tells Melissa he'll accept Stan and Nicole's job offer that following evening. Hands in his notice at work the next day.

# TWENTY-THREE

The difference is that they don't belong to anyone. If I balls it up, break something or somehow brick them, I'm not taking them away from a home or a family or individual that depends on them, has established a relationship with them. I'm not on the hook for them. Plus, they're already… broken. How much worse could I make them by trying to mend them?

Their job is much better than my old one. Better hours, better working conditions. Money is a bit less, it turned out, but enough to live on. You know what, though? It *matters*. That's the big difference.

I'm doing some good in the world. Fair enough, I'm not bringing about peace in the Far East or putting an end to homelessness, but on a small scale, I'm making people's lives better.

No, no-one cared about that in my old job. It was just expected that, when something goes wrong, I rock up, fix it. All as expected. I was just taken for granted most of the time. It's different here.

No, I'm not telling you the address. I'm not doing anything illegal. It might be against the Ellas' manufacturer's license agreements, but I'm not the one who signed those agreements. It was the Ellas' original owners that did that. What I'm doing there isn't relevant to what you're investigating.

I'm not making the problem worse.

It's not hypocrisy. I'm not building new Ellas. And the ones I'm repairing are for purposes that they should absolutely be used for. Live-in carers, for one. They're not replacing anyone's jobs, there's been a shortage of staff in the care sector for decades now, because the pay's so pitiful. Doctors, another. You've got synthetics on the police force doing the jobs that a human police officer shouldn't have to do. Is that hypocrisy?

Fancy that, a nuanced argument.

A lot of people don't see that, get the chance to see that. They get fed the stories they read and see in the news. Sound-bites. Headlines and sensationalism.

Sure, yeah, all those protesters had thoroughly researched each side of the debate, weighed up the evidence for both arguments, and independently settled on the point of view that all AI was bad and that the only solution was to take to the streets.

Perhaps I shouldn't be as surprised as I am that I haven't seen anyone who looks like one of them in the station today.

I can understand a lot of their frustration. I just wish it was directed at the actual people and organisations who were responsible. Not just scattershot, wanton violence and hatred towards anyone or anything that has even the slightest connection to AI.

# TWENTY-FOUR

The anti-AI protests are being covered wall-to-wall by the TV news networks. Wilbur has it on in the background as he works. Watches the overhead shots of crowds spilling through the streets. It's cold, drizzly. Almost as many umbrellas as placards are hoisted above people's heads. They're angry at AI. Angry at the Government. Just plain angry.

Wilbur understands the protesters' frustration. Their resentment. Turns back to the Ella on the workbench in front of him. Got it installed in place of the bed. It rises, lowers, does his back no end of good compared to before.

'You sound disappointed,' says George. George is today's customer. A minor repair. Lost his leg below the knee in a motor collision.

'I'm getting fed up with it. Not the protests so much, as long as they're peaceful. But the rhetoric. That I'm disappointed in.' Wilbur glances up from his work. 'How's your family doing without you?'

'They're getting by. The dad's off work this week, he's

able to look after the kid while I'm in here. You'll be done by the end of today, you think?'

'We should be.'

'I shall let them know.'

Melissa comes in, picks up the crate containing what was left of George's foot and shin. 'I'm doing a scrap run. Do you need me to pick up anything for you?'

'Send Stan,' says Wilbur slowly. Concentrating on a particularly fiddly clip.

'I was thinking you might like some chops for dinner this evening.'

'That sounds delicious. But send Stan.'

'He's already out.'

Wilbur pauses. Looks at Melissa. 'He is?'

'He left an hour and a quarter ago to pick up parts for Heidi.'

'Of course. I forgot it's Saturday today. Can Nicole go with you?'

'No, someone other than you needs to stay here.'

'I'm worried about that lot,' Wilbur says, tipping his head towards the TV.

'I'll be fine, Wilbur.'

'It doesn't need to be you that goes, does it? Nicole knows where to drop off the scrap.'

'I see you're concerned, I'll ask Nicole to go instead.'

'You have to dispose of those parts elsewhere?' says George.

'If we start leaving Ella parts out for the dustbin men, someone's going to cotton onto what we're doing up here,' says Wilbur. 'We drop them off at a handful of different places around town.'

'I can take them out for you,' says George. 'When you're done.' Looks at Melissa. Melissa nods.

'Thank you, George. Let's try and get you up and about before it gets too dark.'

'The dark doesn't present an issue for me, Wilbur.'

'It's not you I'm thinking about,' says Wilbur.

GEORGE IS UP and about in a few hours. Wilbur's wary about letting him take too long a walk before the new parts are bedded in, but George is insistent. Takes the crate, now lidded to hide the contents from prying eyes, heads out into the gathering dusk.

Wilbur and Melissa watch him from the doorway.

'Good work, Wilbur,' says Melissa. 'You're getting pretty adept at this now. He's your sixth in as many weeks.'

'Has it really been that many?'

'Hassan, Theresa, Violet, Alma, Elizabeth. Now George.'

'Wow,' says Wilbur, quietly.

'Are you enjoying it?'

Watches George disappear from sight. 'I am, yes. I wasn't sure I would. Working on Aida was stressful. I think if each one had been that difficult, I might have given you a different answer. But it's been really gratifying.'

'You got another thank-you letter, by the way,' Melissa says, closing the door. Follows Wilbur upstairs into the living room, hands him a tablet.

'Nice job on George, Wilbur,' says Nicole from an armchair.

'Thanks, Nicole. I got another thank-you letter!' Holds up the tablet, doesn't care that he sounds like a child getting a letter in the post for the first time.

He scrolls down the screen, reads the hand-written note sent to Melissa by Violet's new family. Smiles to himself. 'Can you print this one out for me as well, please? Two copies? One for here, one for home.'

'Of course.'

Looks up at Nicole. 'Do you want to read?' Hands her the tablet.

Nicole takes it, spends longer looking at it than she really needs to. Wilbur knows it's a performance put on for him, she can digest the content in a split second. Appreciates the thought, though. 'Aw, that's lovely,' she says.

'Isn't it?' He grins.

'Melissa, look at Wilbur, all giddy.' Ribbing him, he knows. 'All full of himself.' She grins back at him. 'And about time, too, Wilbur.' Stands, opens her arms towards him. 'Come here.' Hugs him.

Wilbur, pressed to Nicole's ample chest, blushes.

'Nicole, leave him alone,' says Melissa.

Nicole laughs, releases Wilbur from her grasp. 'I'm just having fun with him.' Rests her hands on his shoulders. 'Seriously, though, Wilbur, you should be proud of yourself. You're making a big difference to people's lives. That letter proves it, and it won't be the last, I'm certain.'

'Thanks Nicole. That means a lot.'

'Ok, Champ,' says Melissa. 'Shall we head home?'

'I'm ready. We still need to pick up dinner.'

'We can stop off on the way.'

'Nicole, are you going to be ok here on your own?' says Wilbur. 'Have you heard from Stan?'

Nicole rubs Wilbur's shoulders. 'Stan's fine. I'll be fine. You worry too much, Wilbur.'

Pulls his coat on. 'I care.'

Nicole winks. 'I know.'

'See you Monday?'

'I'll be here.'

Wilbur waves farewell, picks up his walking stick, makes his way downstairs and out the door. Melissa locks it behind them.

'You're doing good work, Wilbur,' she says as they walk down the street. 'I'm proud of you.'

'It's good work to be doing.'

'I'm pleased you think so, Wilbur,' Melissa says, platonically looping her arm through his.

IT'S JUST GONE HALF-PAST nine when Melissa says Stan hasn't checked in. Thinks there might be a problem.

Wilbur, sat in his armchair with a book, says, 'What do we need to do?'

'You need to do nothing,' says Melissa.

'Ok, what do you need to do?'

'I need to be here with you.'

'You need to see what's happened to Stan. Make sure he's safe.'

'Nicole will look into it. My priority is still you, remember?'

'If that's true, get your shoes on,' Wilbur says, pushing out of his chair. 'We're going out to find Stan.'

'Wilbur, you're in no state to be tramping across town at this time of night. It's been a full day, you need to rest.'

'I'll pay for it tomorrow, no doubt. But we can't leave Nicole to it on her own. Stan's a friend. We'll find him.'

'Wilbur, I can't stress this enough, you've had enough physical activity for one day. You've worked hard all day, getting George fixed up. It's been a busy week, you need to rest.'

Wilbur ignores her, goes into the hallway. Pulls on his coat, slips his feet into his shoes. Picks up his walking stick. Puts it down again. 'I'd better nip to the loo, first.'

Reemerges from the toilet to find Melissa stood, arms crossed, blocking the front door. 'You're not going out.'

'Melissa, come on. We need to make sure Stan's ok.'

'I wouldn't be upholding my responsibilities to you if I let you go out. You forget why I'm here. What I'm here for. My primary function is to improve your quality of life. What you and I are doing with Stan and Nicole is very much secondary. That the two might overlap is convenient, but don't mistake where my priorities lie. You are staying here, and I am staying here with you.'

Wilbur leans on his walking stick. 'Melissa, you've improved my quality of life more than you could possibly know. More than I could ever have imagined. You've given me a job I care about for the first time since I left the Army. You've helped me improve my health and fitness. I'm walking about with this thing,' Wilbur says, gesturing with his walking stick, 'even though I need it less now than at any point in the last four or five years.'

Melissa, patient. 'Wilbur, take off your shoes and coat and go and sit down.'

Wilbur takes a step towards the front door. Towards Melissa. 'You've given me something to care about. You've got no idea how much I needed that.'

'Wilbur, this is objectively unwise. You are in no fit state to go out tonight looking for Stan. Your wellbeing—'

Holds up his hand. Forceful now. 'No. I'm going out and you're going to come with me. Stan needs you more than he needs me right now because you can find him, and if the only way you're going to look for him is if I go, then I'm going. Melissa, everything you've done for me has led up to this. This is about something bigger than just me. What you and me and Stan and Nicole are doing matters.' Stands in front of Melissa, looks her in the eye. Determined. Can't remember the last time he felt this certain. It's invigorating. 'Ok?'

Melissa purses her lips. 'Ok.'

THEY TAKE the train across town, look at the news reports on Wilbur's phone to see that the large protest has fragmented. Smaller bands of protestors are rioting, causing damage across different parts of town. A taxi takes them in silence the few streets to where Melissa believes Stan to be. They drive past knots of protesters, threes and fours and fives, most dressed in dark clothes, faces covered. Silhouettes moving in front of illuminated shop windows. Theirs is the only car on the roads.

Wilbur exits the taxi. Sniffs. 'Smoke.' Looks up, can't see anything but black. 'And a helicopter nearby.'

Melissa, by his side. 'And at least two drones I can hear. This way.' Leads him further down the high street, round a corner, to a shoppers' car park. It's small, lit by harsh white streetlights and overlooked by council flats with dark windows. A car is burning.

'Any ideas?' says Wilbur. Something in him from his army days keeps him composed.

Melissa points to a cluster of four-wheeled commercial bins in the corner. 'Let's try those.'

The bins are metal. Battered. Paint missing in patches. Wilbur props his walking stick against the side of a bin, lifts the heavy rubber lid, recoils at the smell. Opens it wider to allow enough light in to see. 'Just rubbish.'

Melissa, checking another bin. 'Nothing here.'

Wilbur moves to the third bin, hears a crash from somewhere behind him. Turns, looks at four dark-clad figures walking past the car park. They have the swagger of those who know they're up to no good and can't believe their luck, thinks Wilbur. They either don't notice or don't care about him and Melissa rooting around the bins.

Lifts this bin lid, stench the same. There's a body in this one, though. 'Shit,' says Wilbur under his breath. 'Melissa. Stan.'

She comes to his side to look. Stan's body lies on top of the black plastic bin bags. Well, his torso does. His arms and legs are missing. There's a dent in the side of his head.

'Shit,' says Melissa.

Wilbur glances at her. Hasn't heard her cuss before. 'Are his limbs in the other bin?'

'No. Judging by the lack of fluid on the bin bags, he was separated from them elsewhere.'

'Wilb-b-b-b-bur,' says Stan.

Wilbur barks in alarm, drops the bin lid, stumbles backwards. Bends over, hands on his knees. Feels like his heart is about to burst out of his chest.

Melissa lifts the lid fully, folds it back on itself.

'Stan. Wilbur and I are here.'

'N-N-N-Nic-c-c-cole.'

'I don't know where she is, Stan. She's not on the network. We're fortunate to have found you.'

'Have we lost Nicole, too?' says Wilbur, between breaths.

Stan's chin moves down and up.

'She's nearby,' Melissa says. 'Online still.'

'We'll need a taxi,' says Wilbur. 'We can't take him back to the flat on the train.'

'We'll leave him here for now.'

'What?'

'He's safe in here, out of sight. We can't carry him around while we find Nicole.'

'Can she come to us? If she's still online, can you signal her or something?'

'She's hiding and can't move. Wilbur, stay here.'

'No, you're not going anywhere.'

'Wilbur, stay here.' Firmer this time.

'No.' He can be firmer, too. 'If anyone's in any danger here, it's you, Melissa. You stand out like a sore thumb. You can't go walking around, not on an evening like this.'

Melissa goes quiet. Wilbur knows she's weighing up her choices. Knows that she knows that he's right.

'It's a three- or four-minute walk,' she says. 'If you don't get held up. Use your phone, I'll call you, talk you in.'

'Good. Thank you. Now, if you'll excuse the bluntness, get in the bin. It's the safest place for you right now.'

Wilbur puts his earbuds in. Leaves Melissa and Stan behind him, returns to the high street. Groups of darkly-dressed individuals are still hanging around. Can feel them eying him up. Fortunate that older men with walking sticks aren't on the top of their lists this evening. Wilbur finds the lights in the shop windows reassuring until a loud crash comes from down the street behind him. Sounds like a window being smashed. Doesn't turn to see, doesn't want to dally.

'Just keep walking, Wilbur,' says Melissa in his ear. 'Stick to the side of the street, if you can.'

'Don't worry, I've done this before.'

'That was a long time ago, Wilbur. What's the name of the next road on your left?'

'Acacia Road.'

'Turn down there.'

Wilbur crosses the street, walks down Acacia Road, a residential street with old red-brick terraced houses. It's darker, the streetlights less frequent. No brightly-illuminated shopfronts.

'The second turning on your right should be Kensington Road. Head down there.'

Wilbur hears, doesn't see, a drone pass overhead, towards the high street. Crosses over. No traffic anywhere to be seen. Parked cars. People staying in, enjoying Saturday night in front of the telly.

'You're looking for a garage block, half-way down on your left. I suspect Nicole has forced the lock on one of the doors and hidden herself inside one of the garages.'

Wilbur tries to peer through the night. Can make out the garage block. No-one else around. Lights on behind curtains, the only sign of life. He approaches the garages. Three in a row. Large metal doors on the fronts. All look closed.

'Nicole?' Wilbur says, his voice catching in his throat. 'Nicole?' Louder.

No answer. Taps on the door nearest to him. 'Nicole?'

'Wilbur?'

'Yes, I'm here to help. Melissa's safe.'

The door opens, swings outwards and up.

Wilbur takes a hurried step back. 'Are you ok?'

Nicole steps forward. 'Yes, thank you, Wilbur.' Straightens her hoodie. Sweeps dust from her jeans. Dark colours to fit in. Clothes dirtied and torn, otherwise looks to be fine.

'How long have you been hiding in there?'

'Eighty-four minutes. I spent seventeen before that

running.' She closes the door. Looks left and right, assesses her surroundings. 'Where's Melissa?'

Wilbur taps his ear. 'Phone. Shall we go?'

Three shadows pass across the garage door and Wilbur turns, leans on his walking stick to maintain balance.

'Alright, Grandad,' says one of the three protesters facing them. Faces covered, baggy sweats, baseball hats. Can only tell he's male by his voice 'You're gonna have to let her go. We ain't interested in you.'

Wilbur can't think. Stands there. Useless. Another of the three has a length of scaffold tube held loosely at their side.

'Wilbur?' says Melissa in his ear. He doesn't answer her or them.

'Yeah, that's what I thought,' says the male. 'Fuckin' do him, too.'

In one smooth motion, Nicole sweeps the walking stick from Wilbur's hand, sends it sailing through the air, millimetres from the scaffold tube-wielding one's head. Who flinches and falls. Nicole steps toward Wilbur like she's going to rugby tackle him, hoists him over and onto her shoulder in a fireman's carry before he knows what's going on. Runs.

Feels to Wilbur like he's never moved faster as Nicole sprints down the road. He tries to talk. Can't. Remembers practicing this very same drill a lifetime ago. He could never run this fast with a comrade on his back. Even when their blood was trickling down his neck.

'Wilbur, what's happening?' says Melissa.

They're turning back on to the high street, about to head to the car park. Except they're trapped. There's a line of police on one side of them, spread out across the street, all helmets, riot shields and batons. Protesters lined up on the other side, all bricks and stones and pipes and vitriol. Nicole comes to a halt between the two, Wilbur over her shoulder, to a chorus of whistles and barely-intelligible verbal abuse.

Wilbur doesn't see the first brick fly, but he does feel it graze the back of his thigh. 'Melissa, stay where you are, don't come out,' Wilbur says, barely able to make himself heard.

The protesters move first, breaking into a run. The police brace themselves. Nicole and Wilbur are caught in the middle. Nicole turns, runs towards the police line. No gap opens for them.

'Let us through,' says Nicole with infinitely more composure than Wilbur is feeling.

The police officers don't acknowledge her, she starts moving parallel to the line, looking for a gap through. There is none, except maybe at the end of the line, where it butts up against the shop fronts.

The wave of protesters hits before she gets there.

Nicole stumbles, falls forwards, spilling Wilbur into the line of police. The protesters trip, fall over them. Wilbur feels feet on his arms, legs. Trodden on, fallen on. Curls into a foetal position, wraps his hands over his head. Closes his eyes.

A hand grasps his collar and pulls. Strong. He tries to look but can't, is dragged bodily through the gap between two police officers' legs. It's Melissa. He's panting, shaking, can't speak. She drags him to the side of the road, props him up against a bin. Checks him over. He sees her mouth move, she's talking to him, he can't hear her.

Sees Nicole crawl through the police line, get to her feet. Thankfully whole.

The police line breaks when an officer falls. The resulting gap is the undoing of the line as a whole, as protesters surge through. The line of police officers breaks, splinters into smaller groups, standing back-to-back. Sirens cut through

Wilbur's aural murk. A van with flashing blue lights shudders to a halt nearby, disgorges more officers who run to support their beleaguered comrades.

'Wilbur.'

'Wilbur.'

'Wilbur.'

He looks up into Melissa's face.

'Wilbur, we need to go. Are you able to walk?'

'I think so. Help me up.'

He tests his legs. They're shaky with adrenaline. 'Stan.'

'Yes.'

Melissa and Nicole watch as he takes a couple of faltering steps. Steadies himself on the bin. Melissa comes to his side, slips his arm over her shoulder, provides support. They're slow but they're moving. A brick shatters on the road nearby.

Then another. Followed by a glass bottle that explodes into fragments. Then they're jostled to the ground. Nicole spins, arms outstretched, tries to catch him and Melissa. They fall anyway. Wilbur rolls onto his back, props himself up. It's the male from earlier, and the one with the scaffold tube. The scaffold tube swings at Nicole's head. She ducks, she's fast. Melissa crouches over Wilbur protectively.

Nicole steps forward, shoves Scaffold Tube, who stumbles backwards into a police officer trying to restrain another protester. Scaffold Tube's arms windmill, trying to keep balance. Inadvertently clocks the police officer on the side of the helmet with the tube. The officer sprawls, witnessed by a comrade who runs over, strikes Scaffold Tube on the arm with a baton. The tube drops, the officer strikes again, this time on the back of Scaffold Tube's legs. Scaffold Tube's mate runs at the officer, a stone in hand, swings at the officer's head. Strikes a glancing blow.

Melissa pulls Wilbur to his feet. A teargas grenade skittles past spewing clouds. 'Come on, Wilbur,' Melissa says, as more police arrive. Equipped with firearms now. Teargas launchers, evidently. Rubber bullets, too, Wilbur worries

'Stand in there,' Melissa says, pushing Wilbur into a shop doorway. 'Nicole and I will retrieve Stan. Don't go anywhere.' Holds her finger up, admonishingly. Wilbur nods, could do with a moment or two to collect himself. Nama-fucking-ste.

Leans against the doorframe, stares out at the melee going on in the street. The police are gaining the upper hand. Officers hold protesters prone on the ground, bind their wrists with plastic ties. Start re-organising themselves, re-forming their line. Help injured comrades away from the danger.

Melissa and Nicole call out loudly. Wilbur pokes his head out from the doorway to see them at the turning to the side street a short distance away, pushing a shopping trolley containing Stan's torso. Clever.

He's not the only person who's noticed them. Wilbur sees Scaffold Tube's friend sprinting towards Melissa, shouting something unintelligible. Sees Melissa and Nicole turn, too late. Male protester barrels into them, swinging a brick.

Wilbur hobbles out into the street, no way he can get there in time to help. A nearby police officer fires rubber bullets in the opposite direction. Wilbur grabs the officer's firearm, disarms him the way he was taught a long, long time ago, pushes the officer away. The officer stumbles on a bottle, falls over. Wilbur holds the firearm to his shoulder. It feels heavier than he remembers. Muscle memory's still there, though. Leans into it, lines up the shot. Estimates the range at thirty metres. Pulls the trigger. Doesn't remember the kick being as painful on his shoulder as it is. Sees Scaffold Tube's friend plucked sideways as if by an invisible giant.

Wilbur drops the firearm, hobbles the distance to Melissa and Nicole as quickly as he can. Melissa's on the ground. Wilbur feels fear pooling in the pit of his stomach. Hasn't felt that in a long time, either. Nicole's crouching over her.

'Melissa, what happened?'

'Wilbur—' says Nicole, as Wilbur crouches at her side, shouting Melissa's name.

Melissa's ear is missing, a mess of skin and blue fluid in its place. But that's all. Wilbur breathes a sigh of relief. 'It's ok, Wilbur. I managed to avoid the worst of it. Something hit him, I didn't see what.'

'I shot him,' says Wilbur, panting. 'Rubber bullet. We're all here now, let's go.' Looks to his right, Scaffold Tube's friend is sprawled in the street. Not moving. Wilbur isn't minded to care about him. Turns to Melissa and Nicole. 'If I climb in the trolley with Stan, can you push us both?'

# TWENTY-FIVE

Is that the part of all this that you find hardest to comprehend? That I placed a greater value on the life of an Ella than a so-called fellow human?

Well, why wouldn't I? He means nothing to me. In fact, he'd already threatened me with physical violence by that point. He's endangering someone I care about deeply. Who is an incredibly important part of my life. I was acting in self-defence. He deserved what he had coming.

Remorse? Look, I wouldn't wish harm on anyone. I'm sorry that it injured him as severely as it did. But he put himself in that position, no-one else.

And when he's released from hospital, I'm assuming he'll be charged with the various crimes he committed.

If I hadn't shot him with the rubber bullet, he would have seriously harmed her. Possibly the others, too.

It's not that easy to replace her. You know how they work, right, the memories and all that? A new one wouldn't be the same. Just as you wouldn't be the same person if you lost your memories instantaneously. I'm not going to get into nature versus nurture, but even you have to admit that you're shaped by your experiences. Ellas, they're the same.

They do have a cash price associated with them. And if I was well off enough, sure, I could probably go and buy one that looked identical. But I'm not, and even if she looked the same, she wouldn't *be* the same.

You're missing the point.

You know why there aren't any of them in the Army? In the infantry, specifically?

Because they're so expensive. Yes, they can march further, faster, and shoot a gun with more accuracy. But they also cost more than a raw recruit's salary for the first couple of years. And they're just as vulnerable to bombs and bullets as humans. And you know what the kicker is? There's no shortage of kids ready to sign up and enlist. And while the country's content to throw young men into the Army because they're less expensive, you can't sit there and tell me my judgement of the relative value of a human's life versus an Ella's is wrong.

# TWENTY-SIX

A pair of police officers show up at Wilbur's front door the next morning. He's not finished his breakfast yet. He's not altogether surprised, either. Tells Melissa, 'I'll get the door.'

The officers introduce themselves brusquely. Ask Wilbur his name. Tell him they're arresting him. Suspicion of inflicting grievous bodily harm. Give him the option of being led out to the waiting police car without handcuffs.

Wilbur asks, 'Can I put my shoes and coat on first?'

'Go on,' one of the officers says.

'Can I have a minute alone, to say goodbye?'

'No,' says that same officer, closing the front door, shutting them in. 'But you can say goodbye.'

The other pushes past Wilbur to stand in the living room where she has a view of the kitchen. Hand resting on a taser in her belt.

Wilbur shrugs, returns to the kitchen.

'Try and finish your breakfast,' Melissa says, softly. 'It sounds like you'll need to keep your strength up today.'

Wilbur sits. Looks at her. Smiles. 'Thank you.'

Melissa sits opposite him at the little table. 'The police car's parked just outside. There's a van from Autonomi Industries next to it.'

Wilbur breathes in deeply. Breathes out. 'I was hoping we'd have a little more time before they showed up.'

'I know.'

Wilbur pushes his food around his plate. Clears his throat. 'Listen—'

'I know,' says Melissa. Reaches across the table, takes his hand. Squeezes it.

Wilbur looks her in the eyes. Thinks, she does, you know. In her way. Takes a final mouthful of breakfast. Finishes his coffee. Stands. Extends his arms toward Melissa. 'Before I go.'

She stands. Allows him a hug. Feels her arms embrace him. Feels safe. Feels warm. Feels like home.

He steps back, checks the bandage around her head. 'You'll be ok.'

'Here,' Melissa says, handing him his phone. 'Just in case.'

Wilbur smiles, tucks it in his pocket. Turns to leave the kitchen. Go and put his shoes on.

Melissa sits back down. 'I'll be seeing you, Wilbur,' she says.

# EPILOGUE

'My last question, then I'll leave you in peace,' Marjorie says. It's near the end of the eight-minute video on the MVA's YouTube channel. Wilbur remembers it taking a lot longer than that to film. Probably forty minutes in at this point.

First time he's seen the video. Hadn't wanted to be reminded of what he'd lost while in prison. He watches Marjorie lean in, an interested expression on her face. 'I understand from Autonomi Industries that you have a particularly unique connection to Melissa, your Enhanced Living Assistant. Would you tell us more?'

He can see himself tense on screen. Hadn't expected that question, caught him off-guard.

'Well, a decade or so ago, Katherine – my late wife – and I were struggling. Financially. And we heard there was a tech company offering cash payments if they could scan your face. Katherine thought it might be an easy few quid, she applied and sent a photo of herself in.'

Watches himself settle in the armchair. First time all interview he'd felt comfortable. 'She was a beautiful woman, my

Katherine. Not in the way you see on TV or the magazines in the supermarket, all made up. Just… naturally beautiful.' Can see his eyes twinkle as he reminisces on-screen. 'Didn't need makeup to look incredible. Katherine passed muster and was invited by the company to have her face scanned. She got paid, not lots, but enough to pay for the week's food shop.

'We didn't think any more of it. A couple of months later the company approached Katherine again, asked if they could buy her image and likeness rights. Her face, basically. They wanted to buy the rights to the way she looked. Offered us a much larger sum of money in return. We discussed it, what little there was to discuss. We needed the money, Katherine signed.'

'And that company was…' Marjorie says, leading him on.

'Autonomi Industries. Apparently, they'd found it difficult to create realistic facsimiles of human faces without upsetting people who thought their face had been copied without permission and given to a synthetic. They'd been sued, I think. They figured if they bought the image rights to individuals and used their exact likeness, it would get around that and be less costly.'

'And all these years later, you've been reunited.' Gushing smile.

Wilbur knows what's been cut from the video on YouTube. The initial confusion. His faltering, 'No.' Him saying, 'Melissa is not my wife. She is incredible, she's turned my life around, but she could never replace my wife.' Thinking, not saying, Why do you think I was in such a mess to begin with? Getting upset, unsure if he's angry or saddened or maybe both, rising from his chair. Melissa placing her hand on his shoulder to calm him down.

No. None of that in the video on YouTube. Instead, cuts to

Wilbur smiling serenely, before fading to a slow-motion shot of the Union Jack flag fluttering in the breeze, the MVA logotype superimposed over it.

None of that.

He pushes up from his old armchair, looks around himself. The flat is exactly how he remembers leaving it. It's been an easier day than he was expecting. The place has been empty for over two years, but there wasn't a speck of dust to be seen when he let himself in the front door. Had picked up milk, bread, things to make sandwiches with on the way home. Only to find cupboards full and the fridge, not only switched on, but fully stocked with food, too. Glances out the window, realises it's dark already. Flips the living room light switch, limps to the kitchen. Physio's been lacking these past couple of years.

In the middle of making himself a sandwich for dinner, the doorbell rings. The old butterflies return. Hobbles to the front door, urgently pulls it open. Grins. 'You've evidently got your keys still. You could have let yourself in.'

'And likely have given you a heart attack, Wilbur, if you see me suddenly appear out of nowhere,' says Melissa. Pulls the deep hood of her rain cloak back, steps inside.

Wilbur looks into that familiar face. Feels the last two-and-a-quarter years start to lift from his shoulders. Gestures to the side of her head. 'May I?'

Melissa tilts her head to the side, pulls her hair back.

'Lean down a bit.' He gently turns her chin. Ear's still wonky from that night. It didn't heal evenly. He wasn't around to make sure it did. He's not going to do anything about it now, though. It's hers.

Uniquely hers.

. . .

'YOU'VE BEEN BUSY,' Wilbur says, looking around him at the new flat.

'We've got work to do, Wilbur. You've been sat around doing nothing for the past couple of years.' Gives him a nudge with her elbow. Playful. Cheers him. 'I assumed you'd be keen to get started.'

He nods. This place is like the last. Spotlessly clean. Same ad-hoc collection of hand-me-down furniture. 'There must be customers coming and going at all hours downstairs. That's clever.'

'Don't get any ideas.'

'I've not had a drop of alcohol pass my lips for over two years. One sip and I'd probably be flat on my back.'

'I'm definitely locking the front door when you're here, then.'

Wilbur goes to the bedroom door, opens it. Curtains are closed but he can see the three human forms, each under a sheet, lying next to each other on the bed. 'You *have* been busy. Did you manage to rescue anything from the old place?' Trolley at the foot of the bed with boxes and cables in it.

'I managed to save the transfer machine. The pale grey box, you call it.'

'Anything else?'

Shakes her head. 'Just a few odds and ends. It's all there on the trolley.'

Wilbur walks quietly to the trolley, looks through the bundle of cables. There's an empty drive. 'That's ok. We can start over.' Takes off his coat.

'You don't want another day or two to reacclimatise? I was teasing you just now, you know.'

Grins, passes her to hang his coat on a peg by the front door. 'I'd like a cup of tea. Is there any milk?'

'I put some in the fridge yesterday. I'll put the kettle on.'

Picks up a dining chair from the kitchenette, moves it to the bedroom, next to the pale grey box. Pulls the empty drive out of the jumble. Spends a few minutes plugging everything in. When she returns with a mug of tea, he pats the seat of the chair. 'Come. Sit.'

She puts the steaming mug on the windowsill, sits.

He connects sensors to fingers. 'Ready?'

Looks him in the eye. 'Always, Wilbur.'

Pauses for a moment, her hand in his. Gives what he thinks is an imperceptible squeeze. She squeezes back. Properly. He smiles, releases her hand. Pulls a pen from the mess on the trolley. Carefully, in wobbly capital letters, writes *MELISSA* on the side of the empty drive. Connects the drive to the pale grey box.

Takes a deep breath.

Squeezes her fingertip.


THE END

---

Thank you for reading Project Aida. If you enjoyed reading it half as much as I enjoyed writing it, I'd love for you to write me a review.

Leaving me a review, even if it's just a star rating or a single line, really makes a difference to indie authors like me. It helps people find my writing and lets them know what you enjoyed about it.

And if you're interested in your own ELA and signing up for my newsletter, please visit autonomi.industries

---

## DIGNITY THROUGH TECHNOLOGY, DELIVERED WITH HUMANITY

In an era where technology and compassion intersect, Autonomi Industries leads the way in revolutionising home care for seniors and individuals with unique wellbeing requirements.

Our Enhanced Living Assistants are changing how people experience ageing in place, providing unprecedented levels of independence while ensuring safety and companionship.

### Find out more and sign up for updates at autonomi.industries

# NEWSLETTER SIGN-UP

**Wilbur and Melissa aren't done yet.**

Sign up to my newsletter for updates about the next chapter in their story, as well as exclusive short stories and other goodies.

**Sign up at**

**www.autonomi.industries**

# ABOUT THE AUTHOR

**Michael Abolins** lives near Bath, England, with his wonderful wife, daughter and two dogs. He spends his days managing a team of talented UX writers, his lunchtimes running in the countryside, and his evenings indulging his many hobbies, one of which is dreaming up new stories.

www.ingramcontent.com/pod-product-compliance
Lightning Source LLC
Chambersburg PA
CBHW010342170726
48283CB00009B/2921